The

Marker

Roy Dean

ISBN-13: 978-0-578-18673-3

I must give special thanks to Jesus Christ, without whom, I am nothing. I also have to thank D.J. for keeping me encouraged throughout this project. Finally, this work is in memory of King Red and that final ride we never got to take.

Prologue

The Dolores River runs swift and cold on its journey to meet the Colorado. Starting as a trickle of melting snow, it gains volume and speed as it falls through gray, twisting, canyons of towering granite cliffs. Walls of stone imprison the river for much of its length; making crossings few and dangerous. Will and Anna Prentiss paused at one such crossing. The stream was dark, heavy with sediment. Ominous waves white-capped over the submerged rocks. The waters were more menacing than they had been in some time.

"Honey, this doesn't look right," Anna protested; her voice scarcely containing the anxiety she felt. The previous two years had been difficult for the young couple. They had tried to make a life for themselves in the farming community of Dove Creek on the western edge of Colorado. The alfalfa crop brought in a little money, but did not offset the pitiful corn. Will's stud bull did not survive the harsh winter, so he sold the remaining two cows to his neighbor.

Will hated to admit defeat, but family must come before pride. After many sleepless nights he'd decided his beloved Anna deserved better, so he loaded what he could into their wagon and headed north, the most precious cargo being their three-month-old daughter. The grandparents in Grand Junction were going to be thrilled to learn of her.

"We got to try it," replied Will. "The next place to get

over is a day away, and the baby needs a doctor." The infant began running a high fever the day before. Nothing they had tried brought relief, and for the past hour she was listless and cried only faintly.

"Tell you what," suggested Will, "I'll leave you and the baby here in the wagon and take the horse across first to see how deep it is."

"Please be careful, Will. I tell you it don't look right."

"Don't fret. When I get over I'll tie the rope to one of those trees and use it to help guide the wagon. Our child needs help and there's a doc about a half day away , but we got to get across first."

Will loosed the horse from the harness and coaxed him into the stream. The frigid water startled the nervous animal. Walking slowly and picking its path cautiously, the horse started across.

Something moved! Whether it was flotsam or fish, something brushed the horse's underside. Immediately the frightened beast reared and threw its rider. The icy water took Will's breath away. Before he could recover, the flaying hooves of his mount struck him. As the flounder horse began to drift downstream, Will, unconscious and bleeding, sank below the surface and was carried away, out of sight.

"Will!" shrieked Anna. Terrified and without thinking, she bolted from the wagon and raced for the river. Reaching the wet gravel shore, she lost her footing and slid into the roiling torrent. In her long dress and layered petticoats, she never had a chance; the violent flow claimed her also.

In less than a minute it was over. The river was alone again with its flood song, which the haunting winds carried out of the narrow canyon, along with the faint cries of an orphaned infant.

ONE

Sunrise in the San Juan Mountains: the predawn gray gives way to increasing rays of sunlight that seem to penetrate even the darkest recesses of the remote canyons. Chipmunks scurry to find an early breakfast while avoiding the ever-vigilant red-tailed hawks that are about the business of acquiring their own meals. As the sun rises above the peaks, the forest comes to life with predator and prey carrying out the day's routine.

Daybreak on a clear morning was awe-inspiring to those who took the time to give it notice, but Bunckus and Gilbert never gave thought to such things. The new day caught these two as busy as usual, digging, picking, and poking in any place they thought gold or silver might be hiding. The locals referred to them as the "Stick Brothers," since these were the only weapons the town council agreed they could possess. The residents of nearby Silverton, Colorado cringed to see these two come to town. Mercifully, the boys only came in about three times a year, and for most this was plenty.

The citizens of Silverton were not the only ones to have their fill of the two. The boys had been invited to leave several places, from Coal Bank to Ouray. Nowadays they spent their time along South Mineral Creek and its tributaries. Spilling from a lake high in the peaks and meandering its way to the Animas River, South Mineral afforded many opportunities for the would be prospectors.

No one in Silverton really knew where the boys came from or when they actually came to the area. The pair just appeared one day. The Saloon keeper in town was oft to quote, "I thank they climbed outta one of them holes up there." From their appearance it was easy to share his sentiment.

Indeed, their humble home was only slightly better than a hole in the side of a mountain. The two did have a cabin, which was actually an abandoned derelict shack that was more of a "shelter in name only" dwelling. Several windows were broken and boarded up and you could view the stars from your bed at night. There was a lean-to attached to the side that provided some shelter for the horses. It was sparse, but home is where the heart is.

Bunckus was the shorter of the two. Though standing five feet two inches tall, he would vehemently argue he was five foot four. He appeared to have a light complexion with reddish-blond hair. Yet, an ever-present layer of grime that had become part of the man made it hard to really tell. His scraggly beard grew as if it had a life of its own.

His clothing consisted of a pair of well-worn overalls with a dirty cotton shirt. His shoes were a bit over-sized and scuffed beyond the point of being able to tell what color they had originally been. The poor, tattered footwear looked to have traversed the entire Oregon Trail.

He had not been blessed with the gift of conversation. With a severe stutter, the inability to form certain consonants, and little grasp of the rules of grammar, dialog with him was entertaining at the least.

Gilbert, his partner, was taller and thinner. He was never to be seen without his homemade hat. It was constructed of crudely tanned leather and stitched together with strips of rawhide. The top came to a point and the brim flopped whichever way the head was turned. From a distance he had the appearance of a Halloween witch having a really bad hair day. He was also very fond of his faded denim jacket. It was as worn out as Bunckus' shoes, with only small hints of the original blue peering out from behind the dust. Even when the boiling desert heat poured down on him, he may remove his shirt, but the jacket went back on.

It was the middle of June, but pockets of snow still clung to colder weather in the higher elevations. As a result, the boys kept their prospecting close to home. Here, Bunckus picked at what he thought was a promising vein. There, Gilbert dug through a mound of rubble higher up the cliff, carefully examining each handful of soil and discarding the refuse over the edge.

"'It wook wike goe," Bunckus proclaimed to himself, as he

often did. Bunckus not only spoke to himself, he answered his own questions and, on occasion, got into intense, self-to-self arguments if he didn't think he'd answered properly.

As he pondered the rock that, apparently, looked like gold, he was assaulted from above. A handful of gravel and sand landed, without warning, squarely on his head. Bunckus immediately flattened himself to the ground, like he had seen the marmots do when they sighted an eagle flying overhead.

As Gilbert continued poking around the ridge, his attention was drawn to a rather promising ore sample. Some minutes of examination revealed it to be only pyrite, a mineral quite common to the area. Pitching it over the side, he searched on.

Lying still and carefully scanning the sky, Bunckus decided that the danger had passed and quickly returned to his exploration. He had no sooner returned to his work than he was struck again with a larger stone.

"Yow!" he cried, as he dove for cover in a nearby aspen grove. Rubbing his head and peeping out from among the close-knit branches, Bunckus was sure something was out there.

Meanwhile, Gilbert, slowly working his way around the

ridge, came upon a hole. It looked like many of the test pits miners sometimes dug to explore a promising site. Since his head would not fit in, he had to search it by hand.

What he had no way of knowing was that, at the end of this hole, out of sight of the rising sun, a badger had just settled in for a small rest. His previous night's foraging had not been overly successful and now the animal just wanted to sleep.

It is a curious thing about badgers. The Almighty, in creating them, seemed to have left out any measure of patience within the creatures. They are, on their best days, inhospitable; being awakened by the groping hand of an uninvited guest made them much less so.

One thing few people know about badgers is that once you grab one, they are not very easy to let go of. Gilbert, the poor fool had just become keenly aware of this fact. Feeling the creature on the end of his hand, he withdrew his arm from the hole with animal attached. With all the desperate effort he had, he tried to let go of this ill-tempered creature. The two of them scuffled across the mountainside for, "about three 'ires," as Gilbert would later recount. During one, brief moment of respite, he was able to get a foot under the varmint and kick it over the edge.

Meanwhile, as Bunckus had been distracted from his work by an assault from some unseen assailant, he decided it would be a good time to answer that call of nature he had been ignoring all morning. The aspen trees around him seemed as good a place as any, so he dropped his one overall strap and squatted to take care of things.

He had not quite gotten into position when he was assailed from above. This time it was serious!

The airborne badger that Gilbert had so desperately kicked over the cliff landed squarely inside Bunckus' lowered britches and proceeded to bite and claw everything that was exposed.

"Owe! Gibbert, hep hep tumpin' got me. Gibbert, hep hep!"

It was not exactly clear which one was trying to get out of the overalls the most, but, in the end, Bunckus won. He left his possessed clothing and ran to the cabin for his stick, hating himself for having left that morning without it. He retrieved his weapon and was returning to reclaim his pants when he ran into Gilbert, scratched, bleeding, and still wide-eyed from his encounter with the badger. Gilbert did not think it the least bit odd that Bunckus was clad only in shirt and shoes.

"Bunckus," he screamed, "You oughta seed tha thang what attacked me up 'are. It had teeth and claws and more teeth and fighted like a bear."

"Oh, I ah I ah I cheed it."

"It had stripes and could scratch and bite all at tha same time and…"

"An an an it could fwy too, anit anit got my bwitche"

The stick brothers once again banded together and went on the hunt for a pair of ragged overalls wrapped around a severely agitated badger.

TWO

Sitting in a chair with his feet propped on the front porch railing was something John Law had dreamed of many times while riding the trail. John Randall Law (yes, his name really was John R. Law) was getting used to retirement. Long days bent down in the saddle trying to follow signs without being seen by your prey, and cold nights on the ground sleeping with one eye open can take a heavy toll on a man. His hair was all silver now and his gait had lost a bit of the swagger, but even at sixty-three he was still a formidable adversary. With a name like his, it just seemed natural to be a peace officer.

John started chasing bad guys as a deputy in the Oklahoma territory. When U.S. Marshall, Erick Carlson, was killed in an ambush John had been chosen to fill the post. His first order of business had been to round up the murderers of his mentor and hero. To the best of his knowledge he had gotten them all.

John's defining characteristic as a law officer was his devotion to duty. He was dogmatic that a promise made was a promise kept. His father taught all of his children that a man was only as good as his word, and John's word was his bond.

It had been over three decades since John took to wearing the badge, which was now tucked away in an old cigar box, along with his handcuffs. His guns were hanging in the closet by his bed, and his boots were propped on the porch. Retirement was not all peace and quiet though. The former man hunter had completed every chore he could find, and the ones his wife came up with.

His beloved bride, Joan, was a woman of rare beauty. She carried her petite frame with eloquence and charm, and her soft blue eyes still caused John's heart to flutter as the day he first saw her some forty-odd years ago.

Living with a lawman had not been easy. All those nights when John was out on the hunt were nights of worry for Joan. The days were not much better; looking for a rider to come and hoping it was the right one. What used to be small crow's feet near her eyes had evolved into full-blown wrinkles. Her once golden locks shined with about as much gray as yellow, but she loved her man. Joan Bekins Law was a woman also committed to promises. She had kept her word given before the preacher to love honor and obey her husband until death separated them.

While her man was out, she tended the home front. The ranch had been a burden in those early years. Sick cattle, sick kids, drought, and Indian raids had often made her wonder if it was worth it.

The ranch was situated a few miles south of Prescott, which at the time was the capitol of the Arizona territory.

She and John loved the place from the moment they first saw it. The hills were dotted with Ponderosa pines with a few oaks scattered in between. A small stream, known as Lynx Creek, wandered its way through the middle of the property. With adequate water and decent pasture, the place seemed perfect for a cattle ranch, and thus far it was a success.

The two sons she had given John were grown now and running the spread, and with all the debts paid off Joan thought to herself, "Yep, I might just prop my boots up too." John was sitting in his favorite chair reading a week-old newspaper story about a man with a buggy that did not require a horse to pull it.

Technology was a hobby of his. He was amazed with telegraph wires and high speed trains, some as fast as sixty miles per hour, and now a horseless carriage. He also read all he could find about a fellow named Bell, who had an invention that was allowing folks to talk and hear one another over wires like the telegraph. What else would this new century of 1900 bring about?

His contemplation were soon interrupted.

"John, are you going to ever bring them rugs back in?" Momma Liz questioned. The question was more command than inquiry.

Elizabeth Bekins seldom had a kind word for her son-in-law. She did not consider law enforcement a respectable profession and wasn't timid about saying so. Elizabeth tried to convince her daughter that a man being paid to wear a gun was no better than the criminals he chased.

Elizabeth moved into the Law household after her husband passed on. She found it difficult to be alone after forty-eight years of marriage, and John took comfort knowing that Joan had company while he was away, but now that he was home, Mamma Liz strained his patience.

"I'm coming with them now," John said aloud. Then more to himself he added, "I wonder if I could stuff her in a trunk and ship her to her sister in San Francisco."

The idea warmed John's soul until he thought harder on it.

"Naw, that would be a terrible thing to do to a freight driver."

Rising from the chair his actions were halted by the sound of a rider coming.

"Marshall John, Marshall John," shouted the messenger.

Hector, from the telegraph office, often brought news to the Law Ranch. It was not unusual for him to ride out, but this was the second time this week. The message seemed urgent.

"Easy Hector, You got a burr under your saddle?" John asked, as he reached for the reins to calm the horse.

"Marshall John, these telegram come for you and Sam say you need to read right away," exclaimed Hector as he jumped from his horse.

You would have thought the man ran the distance from town on foot considering how out of breath he was.

"Alright, let me see," John said as he took the letter. "Go, water your horse, and cool yourself down too. You know where everything is."

"Thank you."

As the weary horse and rider disappeared around the corner of the house, John read the news. It was a message from one of his informants in El Paso; one of many folks that came to owe John debts of gratitude over the years. The message was simple and straightforward:

"Your man left Juarez Tuesday; Headed north."

"I knew you would come back," John said softly. "And I know where you're going."

The man referred to was preventing John from really enjoying his retirement. He was the fly in John's ointment, the cause of many sleepless nights, the one that got away. Five years ago D.H. Miller had slipped across the border into Mexico before being nabbed, and John was not allowed to follow. Five years of bribing rats to watch a rat had finally paid off. Five years of prospecting were over. Now it was time to go for the gold.

Joan was not going to take John's leaving again very well, even though she intuitively knew that her man would go out one more time.

"Are you waiting for me to keel over and die before you bring in those rugs?" Momma Liz questioned again. John bit his lip and retrieved the rugs. The rest of the day was spent consoling Joan about the journey and giving instructions to the boys on running the place. He knew they could handle everything and it made him very proud of his fine, young men.

Daylight the next day found John kissing his wife goodbye again. Joan had packed a single bag with clothes for about a week, ignoring Momma Liz's suggestions to pack everything he owned.

John planned to take the train out of Prescott to the Indian Agency in Gallop, New Mexico. From there he would board another and yet another, all the way to the mining town of Silverton, Colorado.

Memories of the isolated mountain community flowed over him again. His mind replayed the images of the victims. In all his life he had never encountered such barbarism. Three people tortured and murdered in a way that no human could think of. Inhumane acts of savagery were the trademarks of this animal though.

Some folks said that the D.H. stood for "Devil Himself." John still felt a burden of responsibility for those deaths in the San Juan Mountains. He had cornered D.H. in Taos, and somehow the snake had slithered away. The little voice inside reminded John, "*if you had done your job, those folks would be alive now.*"

It was time to set things right. John had discussed the issue with the Federal Judge in Prescott many times. Judge Horn presided over many of the cases that John had given testimony in and, though his sentences were not always agreeable, the two respected each other. The judge ran his courtroom with an iron fist. To him there were no small cases. Each plaintiff and defendant was given his full attention and lawyers on both sides attested to his fairness. Bringing John back out of retirement meant paperwork and time to get things approved. The judge decided that if and when the time arose, he would allow John to go and bring the suspect in as a bounty hunter only. Neither of them cared much for these unregulated privateers, but the judge knew that John would honestly try to bring his man back alive.

The hunt was on!

THREE

The three men stood around the watering trough .The tub was made of wooden planks, tightly nailed together and sealed to hold water. This particular one measured six feet long, about two feet high and was nearly thirty inches wide. It was situated a stone's throw from a water storage tank that was fed by a windmill. A pipe ran from the tank to a valve fastened to one end of the trough. It was neither the carpentry nor the plumbing that held the men's attention this day. The body of the man floating within was the attraction. Bloated almost beyond recognition, with eyes bulging and tongue protruding, it was a ghastly sight.

Sheriff Keating was a man of small stature. He was about five feet four inches tall and weighed in at a trim 125 pounds, yet his sharp mind and indomitable grit made up for any physical discrepancies. He had just celebrated his 42nd birthday, which was, coincidentally, his 15th year as Sheriff of El Paso. Albert Keating took the job when former Sheriff, James Gillett resigned to manage a cattle company. The Sheriff was the first to speak.

"You say your boy found him?"

Beremundo Esperanza was a local rancher. He and his family raised a small number of cattle on a ranch that had been deeded to them by the Mexican government. Mundo had served faithfully in the Mexican Army and the parched, arid wasteland was considered by the state an ample reward for his life of service.

Some people would have thought the ranch an insult, but Beremundo was grateful for what he had. To anyone who was interested, he was quick to proclaim that all he possessed came by way of divine providence.

"Si' Señor Keating. Sergio and me, we just get back from getting all the cows together. It take us three days to find them all. I have big rancheria, you know. I tell Sergio to make sure they drink, but I watch the cows stand by the water, and they no drink. I tell Sergio to go and make sure that the trough has water in it. He come back screaming, 'hombre muerto, hombre muerto.' I come here and see this, and then I go and get you and Señor Clark."

Matthew Clark was an ex-military man. He came to the southwest as a medic with the Cavalry during the Indian Wars and never left. The desert scenery and dry climate suited him just fine. Matthew was born and raised in New York State. The long, frigid winters, being locked in with snow and ice, were distant memories to him now and he liked them that way.

He had the knowledge and skills to teach in any university in the world, but being self-taught, he lacked the all-important credentials. He was not really all that unhappy where he was; being the only doctor in town and working part time as Sheriff Keating's deputy. His spare time was spent in studying and reading. Most any subject caught his attention, and the cadaver in the water trough had definitely done so.

The body's feet were bound together with the rope secured to the bottom through a small hole drilled into the wooden trough. A small amount of tar had been packed around the rope anchors to ensure a watertight seal. The hands were equally bound at the wrist and then tied to the waist. Around the neck a rope held the head. This noose, of sorts, also ran through a hole in the bottom of the trough, allowing just enough slack for the head to barely stay above the water.

"Looks like he has been here for a few days." The Sheriff broke the silence.

"Yes, and someone went to some kind of effort to do him in," agreed Matthew.
"Mundo, does Sergio need that chair to reach the water valve?" Matthew asked the question as he walked slowly around the site.

"No Señor, he can reach it fine."

Matt was interested in the piece of furniture. It was a simple straight-backed wooden chair, the type that was inexpensive and apt to be found in any home or business. The chair was really nothing special, but its proximity to the trough caught his attention. When he finished looking for footprints and other things that didn't belong, he sat down in the chair.

The smell was absolutely repulsive, but Matt sat there and stared into the face of the deceased. From his position it would have been very easy to converse with the man in the water. Whoever had put him in the water had wanted to be up close and personal with his victim.

"Matt, the smell here is enough to gag a buzzard, how can you sit there?"

"Sheriff, I believe our bad guy who did this sat here and slowly tortured this man before he let him die."

"Why's that?"

"Well, notice that the rope has enough slack to let him rise up and keep his head above the water until the trough gets nearly full. Filling it up slowly would allow panic to build as the water level rose. He was able to breathe until the water reached the top. After that, keeping his head above the water would force him to strangle himself against that noose. When he lowered his head to loosen the pressure, he'd be below water."

"So, did he strangle himself to keep from drowning or drown himself to keep from strangling?" asked the Sheriff.

"It doesn't really matter; the poor fellow is just as dead."

"Well then, what was the point in all this effort to kill a

man?"

"Information Sheriff, information. The only reason to do a man like this is to get him to talk."

"How could you pull this off without anybody hearing or seeing it?"

"As far as seeing, I think it was done at night. For the hearing, the dead man here can explain that."

Sheriff Keating was not completely following Matthew.

"Take a look at his mouth, Sheriff. Notice those very faint bruises?"

The body was discolored by death, but upon close inspection, some slight bruising was visible around the mouth and leading to the back of the neck.

"These bruises were caused before the man died. I think from being gagged.

"Well, if he was gagged, how could he talk?" further inquired Sheriff Keating.

"Oh, the gag was removed after the water reached the top," explained Mathew. "You see sheriff, the individual that thought this up was not interested in idle chatter. He did not want to hear any begging or deal making. I think he just sat in this chair in stone silence and waited until the victim realized that telling all he knew was his only hope."

"And after he cooperated, he killed him anyway?"

"Sheriff, the person who did this could not leave anyone

behind to tell what happened. So, after getting what he wanted, he just added a little more water to the tank and patiently waited for the man to die."

"Sounds like one deranged idiot to me."

"No sir. While he might be deranged, he is no idiot. This character is very intelligent and methodical. He thinks things through before taking action. And, once his plans are made, he carries them out without any conscience at all."

"How can you do this to somebody and not feel anything?"

"It sounds incredible to a sane and rational person, but there are folks among us who can carry out horrendous acts with no remorse at all. I have been studying that guy in England that killed those prostitutes. He cut them up like they were slabs of beef, even took the time to dissect them like a surgeon."

"Yeah, I heard of him too, Jack somebody....ah, what do you mean among us?"

"Don't expect the person who did this to be some monster", answered Matt. "The perpetrator of this probably looks as normal as anyone. In fact it is possible that we have already met him and did not know it."

The three men stood for a moment, thinking of what the victim must have gone through and of Matt's assessment of his killer. Sheriff Keating broke the silence.

"Mundo, do you know him?"

"Is hard to tell, but I don't think so."

"Well, we need to get him out of here." The Sheriff turned to Matt.

"Yep," agreed Matt. "Mundo, I've got some canvas wagon covers in the store room behind my office. Go and get one. We'll wrap him up and get him to my office."

"Si, Señor Matt. I be right back."

"Sheriff, I guess we need to find out who he was and what he did to wind up here."

"Yep, and since you like puzzles so much, I'm putting you in charge of this. Whatever you need will be supplied. Just solve this, Matt."

There was a sense of urgency in the sheriff's voice and Matt equally shared the concern. Beremundo left to get the covers while Matt and the sheriff started cutting the ropes to remove the body.

FOUR

Situated in a valley at the foot of Red Mountain, Silverton had started the decline that all such boom towns encounter. Many claims were abandoned and the main street had as many shops closed as it did open. Still, some folks were bent on sticking it out and trade was being carried on as normal as the hard times would allow.

The Red King Mine, one of the larger operations in the area, was still producing small quantities of ore. It, along with a few independent prospectors, kept the mill running.

Hal Thomason, a strong and determined black man, was doing well with his blacksmith shop. Since profits were too narrow for new equipment, the old stuff had to be fixed. Miners had no choice but to bring their items to Hal.

Even though the Emancipation Proclamation was over thirty years old, black entrepreneurs were still few. The people in this isolated mountain community seemed to be more color blind than the rest of the nation. They only cared that the machinery still ran and Hal was especially talented at making parts for the well-worn equipment.

He had come to town ten years ago and had been patching and mending steadily since day one. Silverton welcomed Hal, and for the first time in his life, he felt like a part of something. He had no plans to ever leave.

Miss Sally Mae's boarding house didn't rent too many

rooms these days, so she made up the difference by cooking and doing laundry for folks around town. She was a dear and kind soul to all she met. She and her husband arrived in Silverton in the early days to mine with the other miners.

The first few years were better than they had expected. The mountain produced new veins almost every day and the people spent as if it would never end. But the mines were drying up now and Bill, her beloved husband and best friend, had succumbed to pneumonia two years ago. But, she was still the area's sweetheart. Indeed, she never turned anyone away, and kind words were all she knew.

Mortimer Tillman was another of the early ones. Everyone called him Morty. He had done very well with his bar and gambling hall, The Outcrop Saloon. Morty celebrated with those who had discovered new finds and, likewise, provided liquid solace for those mourning the mother lode that still evaded them. Good times or bad, the liquor flowed. Morty was also the part-time sheriff. His fellow citizens often derided him for jailing the same fellows he helped intoxicate. He took the ribbing in good humor and returned the insults with equal vigor. The small mountain town seldom had any real trouble. Everyone knew and looked after his neighbor, so when the strangers rode in they were quickly noticed.

Two men rode into town late in the afternoon. Nowadays

the only folks that came to Silverton were gamblers, tourists, or thieves. Tourists normally arrived by train. Gamblers dressed better.

It was clear that these men were at home on the trail. Their horses were sleek and well cared for. The beasts walked confidently, every muscle firm and sinews taunt. With eyes alert and ears pricked forward, it was easy to see that these mounts were accustomed and ready for the chase.

The newcomers were uncomfortable being in the open street. They made no grand entrance. After settling the horses with the livery stable, they went to Miss Sally and rented a room. Their only request was that the room has a view of the street.

Unseen by the townsfolk, a third rider was also in the area. Yet, he dared not go into town. After leaving the Mexican border and traveling mostly at night, D.H. Miller was close to his goal.

It had been five years since he had been on the trail and his body was paying him back for the saddle time. As he tried to stretch the stiffness and rub the aches, he mentally retraced his steps. Had he been careful enough? What were the possibilities of someone having seen him? If he had been seen, what should be the course now? Miller constantly checked himself for errors. A mistake could be deadly.

After satisfying himself that all had gone well, he went

over the remaining plan again. Tomorrow he should be able to reach his hidden cache. From there, it was just a simple matter of retrieving it and slipping away unnoticed, leaving just enough signs for the Marshall.

"I wonder if that law dog has made it here yet," D.H. thought to himself as he settled in for the night.

To conserve body heat, he tucked himself under his blankets in a fetal position. The large ponderosa pine at his back would block the wind. It was going to be a cool night, but a fire this close to town would not be wise.

FIVE

Matt and Sheriff Keating delivered the cadaver to Matt's office. They were going to have to get it underground very soon, but Matt wanted to have a final look to see if any clues could be obtained.

"Matt, I don't recognize this poor fellow, and there hasn't been anyone asking about a missing person around here. I think I'll go to the Mexico side of town and poke around."

"That's a good place to look, Sheriff. I want to check his clothes for any identification, and then I'll give the whole body a thorough examination before putting him in the ground."

"Whatever you do, do it quick. The whole place will smell like death before too long," retorted the Sheriff.

Though the body was long past feeling, Matt treated it as gingerly as he would one of his breathing patients. The deteriorated state of the body required that the clothes be cut away. Matt started with the shirt and worked his way toward the boots.

That was enough for the Sheriff. He had seen and withstood many gruesome tasks during his tenure as a border town peace officer, but the site of Matt undressing and scrutinizing the putrid mass on the table was more than he wanted to endure now. He placed his hat on his head and headed to the Juarez side of the border.

He bypassed the local Mexican police, choosing instead to pay a visit to some of his more trusted informants among the back alley saloons. He had nothing against his south of the border compatriots, but if you want to know about a town, you go to those that actually run the town.

His first stop was the leading watering hole in Juarez; an isolated, cut-throat bar known as, El Padron's. The place was owned and operated by a rather portly gentleman known simply as, Padron.

Though nearly 70 years old, Padron still managed his cantina personally; He had heavy bags under his eyes, crowned on top by equally heavy eyebrows. The first impression people got of him was that he never opened his eyes. In truth, the old man seldom missed anything.

Many of his former bartenders had been many caught trying to steal drinks from what they thought was a nearly blind employer. The fortunate ones were relieved of their jobs with only a broken finger or two. The others, rumor had it, were left in unmarked graves scattered in the desert. Longtime residents knew of Padron's demeanor. The newcomers learned quickly.

Sheriff Keating knew Padron was capable of the murder he had just encountered, but did not consider him a suspect. Padron took care of things discreetly. He had neither the patience nor intelligence to carry out the water trough torture.

The sheriff reached the bar and greeted the two guards at the door. He opened his coat, removed his gun from the holster, and handed it butt first to the man on the right. The guards knew the sheriff well and granted him the professional courtesy of not being searched.

Padron did not allow anyone to bring a weapon into his place, especially a law man that may want to enforce a warrant. He was at his usual place sitting on stool at the end of the bar next to the back door. His arms were folded across his rotund belly and he looked to be asleep, but he saw the sheriff enter.

"Padron, I see you're still on duty," greeted Sheriff Keating.

"I have to be on duty to keep these thieves from robbing me poor," he answered, waving his arms toward the customers and employees alike.

"Don't you trust anybody?" questioned the Sheriff.

"I know people too well to trust anyone, even you, Sheriff Keating. I know that you don't come to see Padron for nothing. Who are you after?"

"You're right Padron. I am after someone, but I don't know who. I'm really hoping you can help me."

"And you think that ole' Padron, he know every bad man around, huh?"

"The fellow I'm trying to identify isn't known on my side of the border. I thought maybe he had been from around here."

"Well, what he look like?"

"He doesn't look like much now, because he's been dead for a few days. I need to find out who he was and also who killed him. I was just wondering if maybe there was someone around here that's been missing for a few days."

Padron opened his eyes for a closer look at the sheriff. The question had struck a nerve with the saloon proprietor.

"Well, hombres come and go everyday here. It is hard to keep up with all of them."

"Padron, this poor fellow was killed in such a way that no normal person could think up. I truly believe there's a hombre running loose around here that is crazy and dangerous."

Padron was uncomfortable with the sheriff's interrogation.

"Sheriff, you never drink in my place. Let me get you some tequila."

"No thank you, Padron, I'm still working. But if you can help me catch this killer, I'll come and drink a whole bottle with you. I'll even eat the worm."

Sheriff Keating was not getting the signal, so Padron tried a different method.

"Sheriff you look tired. Let Padron fix you up with some good wine. I just got it in. Good Mexican wine from Monterrey. Wait here, I get it for you."

Padron eased himself down from his perch and waddled off into the back room. It was very unusual for him to personally retrieve a drink for anyone. Sheriff Keating understood the importance.

After a few minutes, Padron reappeared with a bottle of wine carefully wrapped in brown paper.

"I wrap this up so the drunks on the street won't beg you for a taste, and also the police won't take it from you," he said, laughingly, as he passed the package to Sheriff Keating.

"What do I owe you?"

"Nothing," answered Padron with a wave of his hand. "That is for medicine," he said, as he returned to his stool.

"I'm obliged, Padron. Come over and see me sometime."

"Yes, you would like to get old Padron over on your side of the line," the old man replied with a laugh.

Sheriff Keating had to laugh as well. He tucked the bottle into the inside pocket of his coat and left the bar. The guards returned his gun. Silently, he tipped his hat and slipped back across the border to his jurisdiction.

Sheriff Keating hurried back to Matt's office. He was interested in knowing if Matt had learned anything. He also wanted to see what Padron had given him.

SIX

"Bunckus, I'm hungry," protested Gilbert.

"Me me me me too!" replied Bunkcus, "I could eat a kunk."

"Naw, I don't want no 'nother one of them. How 'bout we go to town and git some vittles?"

"We ah ah ain't got any money, Gibbert an what gole we fount a gotta go on 'at marker"

"We might could work for some grub."

"Are we ah ah gonna ah ah take 'a waggin? "asked Bunckus.

"Yeah, we might make us a few dollars haulin' somethin'."

The stick brothers hitched the horses and headed down the narrow road to town. The road was more trail than a thoroughfare. It snaked its way in and out of dense stands of ponderosa pines. Mixed within the towering conifers were the occasional scrub oaks and scattered groves of aspens. A swift, shallow stream accompanied the trail the last few miles, mimicking the many turns as they both wound their way down into the valley floor. Once the main body of South Mineral Creek was reached, the road flattened out and was fairly smooth all the way to downtown. The wild flowers were in full bloom, taking advantage of each precious day of the short summers these elevations allowed.

Flowers bring pollen and Bunckus was overcome with a

36

severe attack of sneezing. After several minutes of almost nonstop nasal expulsions, quiet returned to the travelers.

"Hey, Gibbert, why ah ah why come you 'tut you eye when ah ah ah when you neeze?"

"Cause if ya didn't, ya eyeballs would fall outa ya head, and can ya magine how at would be?"

"Yeah, ah at would ah be bad."

"Can ya jus see your eyeballs laying out there on a ground? They could see you looking fer em, but you couldn't see em ta find em."

Quiet resumed as Bunckus pondered the thought. The boys came into town carefully. They were hoping to avoid any misunderstandings this time. They passed by the blacksmith's shop on the opposite side of the road. Hal watched them proceed. His short, stocky frame and piercing eyes made a foreboding figure, not to mention the two-pound sledgehammer in his right hand.

The first meeting between these three had not gone well. Bunckus and Gilbert had found several empty wooden kegs near an abandoned mine. The boys thought someone in town might buy them, so they loaded them up and brought them in. The first place of business they came to was Hal's. They struck upon a price of three cents each. Hal intended to use them for kindling to get the coals going in the furnace. Bunckus and Hal unloaded the cargo while Gilbert took one of the kegs to check for size. He placed the keg in the opening in the bottom of the furnace. It was a tight fit, but with a few well-placed kicks, it went right in. Hal noticed the activity and stopped unloading to investigate.

"Naw, bwoy! You got to bust it up first," exclaimed the irritated blacksmith. Knowing that the air was being cut off to the furnace, Hal attempted to pull the keg out.

The kegs the boys brought to town were empty black powder containers, remnants of blasting during the early days of mining. Unfortunately, no one noticed that the one Gilbert had stuffed into the furnace still had about a pound of the explosive inside. Hal had his hands on it and was still trying to extract it when it exploded.

The blacksmith shop was completely engulfed with dense black smoke as the combustion belched soot and ashes out of every window and door. The roar was heard all over town and brought folks running to the rescue. A heavy odor of sulfur and singed hair filled the air.

Bystanders thought the worst, but finally Hal came walking slowly out of the smoldering inferno. His clothes were scorched and his eyebrows and beard appeared to have been blasted off. His hair, quite lengthy for a black man, was now all blown straight back and still smoking. He had the look of a man facing a hurricane.

Considering the totality of what they had just done,

Bunckus and Gilbert decided it was a perfect time to leave town; making it a point to avoid Hal and his shop ever since.

SEVEN

The putrid odor met him on the porch.

"Matt, that body has got to go underground and quick," demanded the sheriff.

"Yeah, he's about ripe," answered Matt.

"Ripe! Hell, he's done rotten."

"I got the undertaker's boys digging a grave for him. They will get it done soon. We'll get him in tonight," Matt replied, still staring curiously at the cadaver.

"Do you know more than you did?"

"Not really. He doesn't have any identification anywhere. The only thing I found is eighteen dollars in silver and what looks like a telegraph receipt."

"A telegraph receipt?" quizzed the Sheriff.

"Yeah, it was in his pants pocket. It's faded pretty badly from the water. I don't know how long he carried it before that."

"The eighteen dollars can go to buy you some new tarps. Now, what about the receipt?"

"Like I said, there isn't much here. The message was written in pencil and pretty much washed out, but the date it was sent is written in ink. It looks like it went out this past Monday."

"You think he's been dead that long?" asked the Sheriff.

"Don't know for sure, but from the shape he's in, he

didn't live much past Wednesday."

"I can't take the smell anymore. I'm going to see about the telegraph he sent."

"Sheriff, you know James closed the office at noon today," reminded Matt.

"Yeah, but I know where his second home is," answered Keating.

James Edison had been running the telegraph office in El Paso since it first came to town. He had been trained in the Union Army during the Civil War, and made a career out of tapping the keys. Western Union had put out a call for volunteers to come to the untamed western border towns in those early days. After traveling through the heart of the southern states as a part of General Sherman's entourage, James concluded that Texas couldn't be as bad as where he had been.

He was nearing seventy now, and stooped when he sat or walked. He seldom seemed to straighten his six and a half foot frame out much. Most folks figured he got this way from all those years sitting hunched in his stool working the telegraph.

His hair was gone and his thick wire-framed glasses revealed that his sight wasn't far behind. James was as thin as a telegraph pole his friends said. He always wore a belt with suspenders. These, coupled with his height, hunched back, and glasses gave him a comical appearance.

If he was not in sitting at his telegraph desk, he was likely to be found playing dominoes. There were several bars on the north side of town, but James' favorite was called, "The Salt Lick." It was situated farther from the border and was a bit quieter and accommodated those that were interested in more than just getting as drunk as possible as fast as possible.

James actually drank very little. He had seen it kill his father and, therefore, largely avoided the spirits. No, James came for the games. There were several of James' crowd that played, but with him it was serious.

Sheriff Keating could hear James' high pitched voice before he entered the front door. Even with the noise of the crowd, there was no mistaking him. Tonight the game was going and James was on fire. James was seated at the domino table in the far left corner of the room. The usual crowd was sitting around. They were a mix of businessmen and cowboys from the area. All were about James' age, and thus everyone called this area the "old coots's corner."

"Stop cheatin' boys, the law is here," remarked one of the players upon seeing the Sheriff enter.

"He's probably here to get you for disturbing the peace with that loud mouth of yours, James," added another player at the table.

"Naw, I sent for him to arrest you boys for impersonating

domino players."

"James, can I have a word with you?" asked the Sheriff.

"Sure Sheriff, this hand is over and I done shamed these boys so much they are about ready to cry anyhow."

"Can we step outside?" asked Sheriff Keating, motioning toward the door.

"Take him on down to the jail and question him Sheriff; he's bound to be guilty of something," added a third player. James moved his chair back and walked outside as another player took his place at the table.

"Now, you boys try to remember some of what I taught you," said James.

Sheriff Keating left with James, and the two men walked the short distance to the street corner and turned down a side alley. Once away from the street, Sheriff Keating stopped and turned to James. The expression on his face told James this was not a social visit.

"I want to ask you about a telegraph you sent maybe last Monday. I know you keep records of transactions."

"Yes sir, we keep records for a little while."

"Can we go to your office and look through them?"

"I don't know sheriff. Telegraphs are like mail. They're kind of private. Outside the sender, the receiver, and both operators they shouldn't really be read."

"I'm not asking you to tell secrets, but something has

happened and you are the only link I have to it."

"Link to what?" asked James.

Sheriff Keating looked around, and stepped a little further down the alley, pulling James with him.

"There has been a murder…"

"Murder!" cried James, almost squealing.

"Keep your voice down," reprimanded the Sheriff.

"But I have not done any…nor been involved in any murder."

"I am not accusing you, but the only thing the dead man had was eighteen dollars and a telegraph receipt," retorted the sheriff, trying to control his temper. "Now, I need you to do two things. Come with me to Matt Clark's office and take a look at the body. He's been dead for a few days and he's a pitiful sight, but maybe you can recognize him."

"I am not crazy about dead folks but, I'll look at him."

"Good. Then, we need to go to your place and check on the receipts. Now James, you must keep this just between us for now."

"Let me stop off at the house and tell the wife I'll be working a bit late."

"Alright, I'll meet you at Matt's. Remember, not a word!"

"Has this killing done got you to totin' a bottle, Sheriff?" quizzed James upon noticing the brown package in Sheriff Keating's coat pocket.

44

Keating had forgotten the package from Padron.

"No, this is medicine for a sick friend," he lied.

"Oh, I see," responded James, in a voice that conveyed his disbelief.

"Go on now, and meet me at the doc's office."

"Alright, I'm going."

Sheriff Keating waited in the alley until James was half a block down the narrow street. He then took the bottle from his coat and unwrapped it. The message was short and to the point: **"Behind your office, midnight."**

There was no need for a signature.

EIGHT

The train from Durango arrived on schedule and unloaded its passengers. Silverton had become quite a spot for tourists. The citizens disliked, but tolerated them. They were noisy, demanding, and sometimes just plain rude, but they brought cash. In a town where work was scarce, tourist dollars were always welcome. The warm spring day brought another load of these boisterous folks.

When the train came to a full stop the conductor helped with their baggage, while the engineer saw to the water and wood for the return trip. The brakeman swapped mailbags with the local postmaster and John Law headed to the Sheriff's office.

The city jail was at the north end of town. The locals preferred to have their malefactors out of sight. It was a small, stone structure with an unimposing wooden facade. Were it not for the sign above the door, a person would pass it by without notice.

Once inside though, it was all business. The three cells were small and very secure. Granite was plentiful from the surrounding hills and the builders had not spared. In fact, nearly the entire building was constructed of granite with walls made up of three rows of interlocking blocks. Each block was placed so that it centered on the one next to it. There were no joints in the walls that aligned; digging out meant clawing through nearly four feet of solid rock.

The windows were narrow and placed high, near the ceiling. The bars were mortised into the wall. Removing them would require tearing the walls out also. A prisoner's best chance of escape was to overpower the jailer and grab his keys.

Sheriff Tillman strictly enforced his rule that no one approach the cells without armed back up. A former sheriff had gotten too close one fateful night. An inmate, desperate for freedom, had grabbed him by the throat and took his gun. Since he could not unlock the door while holding the struggling man, he executed the sheriff and made his break.

The incident still haunted Morty and he was determined not to repeat such a horrible event. His rule was firm, "never come near the cell bars without armed back-up."

When John arrived the jail was empty. There were neither inmates nor keepers. John, not overly concerned, left his bag and he went to the livery stable to rent or buy a horse. He was anxious to get started.

The Outcrop Saloon was catering to the usual crowd, plus the newly-arrived city slickers. It amused the everyday crowd to watch the greenhorns belly up to the bar. This was, after all, how they figured real miners and gunslingers did it. The truth was, the locals preferred to find a table and relax as they drank. Most of the daily patrons were hard workers who did not see any need to stand when you could sit.

Morty's lone employee tended the bar. William Barr was referred to as Santa Claus during the off-season. "Willie Bee", as everyone called him, was approaching sixty years of age and looked every day of it. His silver hair was long in the back and gone on the top. The white apron he wore was always filthy and stretched tight over his large round belly. Willie was missing all of his upper teeth, and had a habit of engaging his mouth without waking up his brain. Most folks were used to Willie Bee and ignored his thoughtless comments on every subject that came along. Everyone, that was, except Walter Murray.

Walter was the major shareholder of the Red King Mine. Unlike his partners in the east, he was involved with the daily operations of the business. In a time when many companies were shedding their mining stocks, Walter took a closer look at the west's precious metal industry. He and several of his wealthy associates investigated many of the failing mines on the western slope of the Rockies. The Red King was struggling like many of the others, but Walter thought it had potential.

The mine was located on the northern edge of the Animas Valley. Looking out to the west from the opening of the main entrance, you could view the entire town of Silverton. To the east flowed the Animas River, winding its way southward toward its rendezvous with the San Juan. Smaller peaks, gradually giving way to the mesas and canyon lands of Utah, protected the valley to the west.

To the north, watching over all stood Red Mountain. It earned its name from its orange-colored top, which had been tinted from the rusting iron ores that impregnated the summit.

Indeed, it was Walter's love of the beautiful countryside that had swayed his decision to close the deal. The financial statements and geologist reports were only secondary. He loved the high country and decided that if he was going to spend his time and energy to recover his investment; this was a most beautiful place to do so.

The Red King had thus far been what the investors expected. They had not yet filled their vaults with the precious metal, but they were among the few that were not losing money. The venture was actually making a small, but consistent profit.

Mr. Walt, as he was often referred to, was well known in Silverton and easily recognizable in his business suit and banker's hat. Today he was in the Outcrop watching the crowd and trying to ignore Willie Bee's rambling commentary. The low buzz of the conversation halted abruptly when the Stick Brothers came in.

"I done told you two not to come here again," roared

Willie Bee.

"We ain't here fer no trouble. Wee just wanted to see if we could do some chores fer some grub," replied Gilbert.

"I ain't got anything you can…"
Willie stopped himself in mid sentence, as an idea of devilment swept over him. Bending down behind the bar and fumbling around for a moment, he came up with a shot glass containing a yellow translucent liquid that he gingerly placed upon the counter.

"I tell you boys what, you drank this and I'll see if I can find you something to chew on," his eyes aglow with mischief.

"What is it?" inquired Gilbert

"That's raw panther pee."

The Stick Brothers huddled for a quick pow wow.

"I ah, I ah ah wonner where he fount a panter, Gibbert," queried Bunckus.

"I wonder how he got it to pee in that glass," answered Gilbert.

"You idjits. It ain't real pee. It's just some stuff I got in this morning. Now, one of you drank it down and you'll get to eat."

"I ah, tank I can do it, Gibbert."

"Don't Bunckus. It's liable to make you crazy as a betsy bug."

"Let me twy it."

Bunckus slowly approached the bar, crouching as if to evade being seen by the contents of the glass. He reached up, touched it, and quickly drew back several times, trying to build his courage. After many such attempts, he grabbed the elixir and gently lifted it. His mouth was moving long before the drink arrived.

There were hoots and muffled laughter as the scene unfolded. The liquid was at his lips when the whole affair was halted by the arrival of Miss Sally, carrying a bundle of laundry.

"Willie Bee, what are you stirring up now?"

"Nothing, Miss Sally," Willie sheepishly answered.

"Bunckus is gonna try to drank some panther pee fer sum grub," replied Gilbert.

"You boys don't need to take that poison. I have some leftovers from the breakfast crowd. Go on over to my place and I'll be along directly."

"But, we ain't got no money, Miss Sally," replied Gilbert.

"I got a plenty of chores. Now yaw git along."

Miss Sally knew that the boys would not take charity so, trading leftovers for labor helped her around the hotel and helped the boys maintain their pride. The Stick Brothers left quietly as Sally dropped the laundry on the bar.

"Here are your clean aprons."

She picked up the shot glass and sniffed the contents.

"Willie this is coal oil. You ought to be ashamed of yourself."

Miss Sally' gentle voice and kind demeanor had a way of humbling the most belligerent of people. Willie quietly reached into the till, paid the cleaning bill, and pretended to busy himself wiping the already clean and tidy bar. Picking up her pay, Miss Sally returned to her customers across the street.

Bunckus and Gilbert waited quietly in the kitchen of Miss Sally's rooming house. They were trying to avoid the well-dressed clientele in the dining room enjoying their brunch. When Miss Sally returned, she noticed how uncomfortable the boys felt in the presence of these fancy folks. With her usual charm, she sought to alleviate the situation.

"You know, it's such a fine day out, would you boys like to eat out on the back porch?"

"Yes ma'am, that would be real nice."

"Yeah, hit ah ah purdy day."

"Well, you boys fix your plates. Everything is on the stove or in the oven. There are a few tea cakes left under that towel by the flour bin."

Bunckus' eyes lit up at the thought of those small, slightly sweet, wafers that Miss Sally kept at her inn. They were just flower, vanilla flavoring, and a little sugar, but to boys that lived on what they caught and killed, they were manna from heaven.

The boys rounded their plates, including teacakes, and headed outside for a much sought-after feast. They settled themselves on the lower step and attacked the meal. Bunckus shoveled about half of his bounty down before he had to stop and expel a loud, boisterous belch in Gilbert's direction.

"Dang, Bunckus, watch it."

"I, ah, ah, I torry, but hit good."

"Well, pay attention, if at had been a fart it coulda killed somebody."

NINE

John Law met with the livery manager and rented a horse for his mission. He picked out a three year old roan that had been born in the area. The ten thousand foot plus elevation should not be a problem for such an animal. John re-cinched the saddle and was double-checking the horse's shoes and ankle joints. The steep slopes and narrow trails were demanding on man and beast, and John did not like surprises.

As John examined his ride, his mind was going over plans of action. D.H. Miller could be anywhere in the area. He was certain part of the bullion from Miller's last robbery had been hidden near where the incident occurred. The outlaw had hit a gold shipment from the Ophir Mine, some twenty-odd miles northwest of Silverton. The official ledger recorded $80,000 in gold bars. The gold was returning from the Denver mint where the raw nuggets had been processed into carefully weighed and stamped bars..

Miller had chosen to overtake the wagon where he did because the trail over the pass into Ophir provided cover for the ambush. The crew guarding the shipment would also be less vigilant, since the journey was almost over. What could go wrong this close to home?

Neither the guards nor the wagon ever made it home. Searchers found the mule team shot dead in their harnesses. The strong box was missing. Not far from the wagon lay one of the guards; tortured and murdered. Another teamster was found hanging upside down over what had been a slow burning fire. The youngest of the group was shot in the back of the head. His was the only merciful death.

John continued to formulate his strategy while preparing for the trail ahead.

"He will be sticking to the ravines and heavy forest to hide in," he mused to himself. "It's possible he hasn't arrived yet, or he could have already recovered the gold and left without notice…Or, he could be staring at me from the other side of this horse."

John checked over his ride from nose to tail once more. After satisfying himself that the horse was trail ready, he stood up and clasped the reins. Before his foot touched the stirrup, he was frozen in his tracks.

Miller's day was not going well. He rose early from a restless night and continued his mission. Gingerly, he led his horse down the mountainside in the pre-dawn gray, carefully placing his steps. In the darkness, he missed a small, round stone. It was inconsequential to a man and easily stepped over, but was a disaster for the horse. The beast placed its right front hoof squarely upon the small rock. When it rolled under his weight, the horse tripped and lost its already fragile balance.

D.H. could not see all that was going on, but the sound

told the tale. The horse tumbled head long down the trail, nearly crushing him as it went past. The doomed animal wound up with a shattered front leg and a broken back at the bottom of a narrow side canyon. Now on foot, and a long way from home, Miller left the crippled beast where it landed.

There wasn't time to scour the mountains for an unfortunate miner to steal a mount from. The longer he remained north of the border, the more vulnerable he became. Cautiously, D.H. spent the next five hours working his way into town. There were horses at the livery and expedience was worth the risk.

The old bandit was proud of himself for still being able to evade detection. He had slipped into town without a hitch. Stealthily, he entered the stable and was further pleased with his good fortune. There, at the far end of the barn, stood a beautiful roan stallion, saddled and ready to go. Miller was almost giddy with his luck. He quietly moved across the stable toward the horse.

His euphoria vaporized as soon as he touched the reins. D.H. was preparing to ease the horse out when John Law rose from the other side the saddle. Predator and prey locked gazes for a brief moment.

"That damned law dog," raced through Miller's mind.

John was shocked at the sudden encounter. It had been five years, and from the sight of his old enemy, they were not kind years. The face was thinner and wearing about a week-old beard. The wrinkles were more pronounced, but it was him.

John had lost many a night's sleep thinking of that face. Though he had planned for this moment for a long time, the suddenness of the encounter took him by surprise. He was quickly brought back to reality by Miller's next move.

Without hesitation, the outlaw punched the horse in the mid section. The blow startled the roan and caused it to lunge away from the impact and into the retired Marshall, sending him reeling into the stall behind him. The impact almost immediately reinjured his back. John had fought many bouts with his bad back, and had learned to deal with it. As long as he watched what he did and took precautions, he had few problems. He did not see this coming though, and the pain was intense. By the time he struggled to his feet, Miller was out of sight.

TEN

Bunckus finished his plate all the way down to the bare metal. It was now time for dessert. He carefully cradled the wafer in his hands. It was close to his face. He could smell the vanilla. His mouth was open; the tasty delight lightly touching the edge of his teeth. It was…gone! The teacake was kicked away and trodden under foot by the fleeing D.H. Miller.

The fugitive had scarcely made three steps though, before Gilbert's stick brought him down. Immediately Bunckus was on top of him. He attacked the man with a flurry of fist and feet. He also threw in some clawing and biting techniques he picked up from the badger. Meanwhile, Gilbert worked his stick on everything below the waist; lifting himself off the ground with each blow.

The disturbance caught the attention of Morty, who was finishing up his late morning coffee at Miss Sally's. He and a few other patrons exited the back door to investigate the noise. What they saw could have been humorous were it not so serious. Two bandits appeared to be robbing an unfortunate traveler.

Morty was not surprised to discover Gilbert and Bunckus involved. The sheriff removed Gilbert without too much difficulty. Bunckus required all hands present. They lifted him away from Miller by his arms and legs. He only let go when the piece of shirt he was biting tore away.

This was the first time in D.H. Miller's long criminal career that he was relieved to see the law arrive.

"I warned you two about causing trouble. This time you're both going to jail!"

"Sheriff, he started it. We was a mindin' ire own business," responded Gilbert.

"An an he ah ah he 'tomped my tea cake."

"Shut up, both of you!"

Two bystanders helped the barely conscious Miller to his feet.

"Sheriff, arrest that man!" shouted John.

Morty and the others turned to view the new man upon the scene. John was leaning on the back wall of Miss Sally's place. He was on his feet, but movement was stiff and painful.

"My name is John Law. I'm a U.S. Marshal and I have papers on that man," John said, pointing to Miller. "He is probably armed and you should treat him as extremely dangerous."

The expression on Morty's face revealed his confusion. It seemed odd for him to be locking up the victim, but the man talking to him did not appear to be one prone to kidding around.

"All the papers are in my bag. I left them in your office

this morning."

Pointing to the two men supporting Miller, Morty asked them to escort him to the jail. He then turned to his fellow lawman. "Well," he said, "let's go sort this out."

Morty demanded that the Stick Brothers leave town immediately. They could return when hell froze over or it was eighty degrees in December, whichever came first.

Gilbert and Bunckus looked to Miss Sally. They both felt guilty for leaving town without paying for their meal. As usual, she read their minds.

"You boys go on; we'll get even later."

John walked slowly behind Morty and his two volunteer deputies as they escorted Miller across the street. Miller was still dazed and desperately trying to figure out what had just happened. People milling around town gave little notice to the small parade heading towards the jail. There were two; however, standing at an upstairs window, who were very interested.

"I believe they have our man."

"Yeah and he don't look too good."

"Looks like maybe his horse threw him and drug him a little bit."

"A little? Looks more like a train threw him and drug him a lot!"

John noticed the spectators in the window. He had stayed

alive these many years by paying attention to things that did not fit. It was a beautiful spring day and these two were cooped up inside. If they were businessmen, they should be about their business. Vacationers would be out enjoying every precious moment. These two were content to watch the town from behind curtains. They just didn't fit. John did not know what these two were up to, but that little voice inside was telling him to watch his back.

Arriving at Morty's office, the escorts placed the wounded prisoner on a cot in the middle cell.

"One of you go and get the doc," commanded Morty as he took his pistol from the pocket of his denim coat and placed it in the top drawer of the desk. Morty did not wear a gun belt. He had too much belly in the front and not enough butt in the back to keep one up, so he carried his gun in his pocket.

"Close that door and lock it!" demanded John.

"Now you hold on. I run this place and it's time for you to answer to me."

"I told you, I'm a U.S. Marshal, and that man is my prisoner. I intend to take him to the Federal judge in Santa Fe on the morning train."

"And just what are you taking him in for?"

John paused before answering.

"Were you around here about five years back when a gold

shipment was ambushed near Ophir?"

Morty's expression became very somber. As his mind relived those tragic events, he was amazed at how vivid the memories still were.

"I was here. I went with the group to gather the bodies. We buried them in the hills. There was no way that I was going to let the townsfolk see the condition they were in."

Staring at the wall, but seeing yesterday, the sheriff continued.

"The driver was found upside down over a fire. His brains were boiled inside his head. One of the guards was staked out like coyote bait. His stomach was cut open and his insides were on the ground beside him. It looked like animals had eaten part of him while he was still alive."

Morty was brought back to reality by John's next revelation.

"Well, that fellow there is the culprit. That is D.H. Miller."

Waves of fear and relief swept over Morty. He was relieved to know that the criminal was behind bars, but they were his bars. Morty personally locked the door and put the key in the desk drawer. He also put his gun back in his pocket.

"Let's get a look at those papers of yours."

John retrieved his bag and proceeded to fill the sheriff in on all the details. Morty read through the documents John gave him.

"So, you are actually retired and working as a bounty hunter under the authority of this Judge Horn."

Morty did not comprehend all of the legalities, but if it would get this animal of a man out of his jail, then it was fine with him.

"The only flaw in your plan John is that the train won't be back this way until Monday. So, let me buy you a drink…then we can get you settled at Miss Sally's."

John did not like the news of having to spend the weekend here, but he had to accept it.

"Thanks, but I need to square a horse away at the livery. Then I want to lie down and try to ease some pain."

"Yeah, I noticed you were walking softly. Are your piles bothering you?"

"No, just a worn out back."

Morty pointed to the remaining volunteer. "Go tell the doc to never mind. No need wasting time on the likes of this criminal."

John checked the lock on the cell with Morty. When both were confident that all was secure, they left him alone. John took care of his business with the livery and Morty went to his main interest. The saloon seemed to need much more attention than the jail. Willie was an ample bar tender, but his bookkeeping skills were non-existent.

The two voyeurs watched Morty enter the saloon. One, likely the leader of the two, looked to the other.

"Give that sheriff a few minutes to run his mouth, then go down and learn what you can."

ELEVEN

A short time later, one of the strangers quietly slipped out of the saloon and headed back to the room. His partner was waiting for whatever news he had.

"What did you hear?"

"Plenty! That barkeep can talk the horns off a Billy goat. I don't think he ever shuts up."

"What did he have to say?"

"Well, that was our man they took to jail alright. It seems he had a run-in with a couple of locals and got the worst end of it."

"What was he doing in town?"

"He was trying to steal a horse."

"What happened to the one he had?"

"I don't know, but he was on foot."

"Do they know who he is?"

"They do now. The horse he tried to take belonged to that old crippled coot we saw walking behind the sheriff. He is a retired U.S. Marshal, and he plans on taking Miller to Santa Fe on the Monday train."

"If he is retired, how is he taking charge of a prisoner?"

"It seems he's a bounty hunter now, working for himself."

"Do tell!"

"Yep, so it looks like this trip is a bust."

"Oh, I don't think so."

"You aren't going to break him out of jail?"

The puzzled look on his partner's face demanded an explanation.

"I will go down to the depot tomorrow and get us tickets for Monday. You are going to be too ill to sit in the saddle, so we'll have to put the horses in the cattle car and ride the train home. As I recall, that train stops about three times between here and Durango. We will relieve that old Marshal of his burden at one of them."

"You think I'll be feeling better by then?"

"Oh yeah, you heal real fast, especially when there is gold for medicine."

The two men chuckled among themselves as they continued to perfect their plan. One thing they decided on was the need to exercise the horses. It would not be wise to leave the animals stabled for two days. They decided a trek into the nearby hills and forests would do some good for both men and beasts. After spending a bit of time in their planning, the two had a sudden realization they were starving. A meal, they said, would do nicely right about now. Grabbing their hats from the bedside table, they headed downstairs to see what Miss Sally was cooking.

TWELVE

The sun was beginning to set when Miller came to his senses. Being behind bars was a new experience for him. It was one he did not like. The walls felt as though they were squeezing him in, and the bars seemed to stifle the air around him. He was overcome with a tremendous urge to give in to total panic. As he stood on the cot to test the bars over the window, the sunset caught his attention. He watched the orange ball slowly sink below the peaks and he began to feel that his own life was slipping away into the twilight.

"Nonsense!" he said to himself. "I got by this far on my wits, this isn't anything."

Miller considered himself to be above the average man. After all, he had been outfoxing the law sense his first murder.

A twelve-year-old Donald Henry Miller had been under attack repeatedly from his alcoholic father. Having been knocked down on what would be the final occasion; his hand felt the axe beneath him. He picked it up to move it, and then something happened.

The drunken rage that had been so manifest in his dad's eyes turned to fear. For the first time in Miller's young life, someone was afraid of him. The feeling of being in charge was exhilarating. As he raised the axe, he watched the fear in the old man's eyes intensify. He brought the blade down in the center of the skull and his dad never hit anyone again.

It seemed that murder was the first task he had completed on his own. He was saddened by the sight of the lifeless body and yet enraged at the corpse for making him commit the act. The juvenile killer spent a few more minutes with the axe, hacking away years of anger and fear.

Still in shock over what had just occurred, he had carried the bloody axe into the house where his mother was preparing dinner. He had no intention of harming her. He just stood, staring at her and trying to find a way to explain something that his own mind still could not fathom. It was then that he saw that fear again.

"Why not?" he thought to himself.

After all, she had known about the beatings for years and never tried to stop them. She was looking at him in terror; the same fearful look she used to give his dad.

But now, it was D.H. who was in charge. It was he who caused fear in others. The thrill, the control, the power; they were indescribable. He quickly ended her life also.

The new murderer now had to hatch a plan to cover his deeds. After changing and burning his bloody clothes, he next chose some of his deceased parents' livestock and herded them over the hill and into a nearby valley where a friendly Kiowa tribe was spending the winter in the lowlands.

He watched as the cattle dispersed among the Indians'

stock, then raced his horse to town to recant his tale of coming home to find his folks dead. With all of the skills of an actor trained for the stage, Miller continued to embellish his tale by telling of seeing some Indians making off with his daddy's cows. D.H. was not sure, but he thought they were heading for that broad valley where the two rivers met.

Without questioning the integrity of the young orphan, a group of vigilantes quickly armed themselves and rode out to set things right. They checked the house where the boy's parents lay. They were dead, alright; killed with what looked like a hatchet of some sort. When the group came upon the Kiowa camp, sure enough, there were the missing Miller cattle.

In a rage more befitting wild animals than humanity, the self-appointed executioners descended on the village. The entire tribe was massacred. From a safe distance, D.H. watched the scene unfold. He had not only learned to take life, but he could manipulate others into taking it also. He was completely enraptured with his newfound power. He resolved himself that, now that he was in charge, no one would ever cause him harm again.

Bringing himself back to his current surroundings, Miller slowly regained his confidence. The jail cell was just another obstacle that he would overcome. His body was stiff and sore from the encounter behind Miss Sally's place. He had a cut above his right eye and both legs were bruised. The lower part of his back was extremely tight and movement was not without difficulty, but the circumstances of his arrest were returning to him. The first order of business after he escaped was to find those two who were responsible for ending his flight and make them pay.

Next it would be that meddling Marshal's turn.

"I should have killed him when I had the chance," Miller thought to himself.

He wasn't sure what they had in mind for him, so he proceeded to take control of his situation. He inspected every aspect of his prison. The walls, ceiling, and bars were all secure, as expected. He then sat down on the cot and removed his left boot.

"The fools didn't even search me," he mused.
From a small pouch in the side of the upper, he retrieved a cell door key. He had taken it from a deputy that had the misfortune of stumbling into his path. It was unlikely that it would fit the present door, but why not try?

He worked the key into the lock and gave it a turn. Nothing happened. He would have been surprised if it had. Thinking quickly, and using his boot as a hammer, he pounded the key until it broke. The key sheared even with the face of the lock, blocking the mechanism. He could not get out, but they could not get in either. They would not be taking him anywhere without his being a little better prepared.

The action was insignificant, but at least he felt some relief from the anxiety of not being totally in charge. He lay back on the crude bed and began working out several scenarios of what might lie ahead. Waves of panic continued to sweep over him, but he maintained his composure and kept his mind busy. He was certain of escaping. It was just a matter of figuring out the details.

THIRTEEN

The dining room was crowded. This Friday night was especially busy. The early spring weather had drawn the tourist crowds in prematurely. Miss Sally struggled to keep up with their demands. For most of these folks Monday would come too soon, but to Sally it could not get here fast enough. She often wondered whether the crowds were getting more obnoxious or whether she was just getting less patient in her old age.

As the days and years grew on her, she seemed to increasingly regret having not had children of her own. It wasn't because she and Bill hadn't tried. They had, indeed, given it their best go. She blushed sightly as she recalled some of those attempts. No, despite their efforts, the Almighty had not seen it within his will to bless them with children.

She wasn't bitter by any means. Her thinking was that, in life, you play the cards you're dealt. There was no benefit in living in the past. She had no children to raise so, she tended to adopt everyone else as her own. Tonight was no different. She was attending to the needs of the patrons as if each were her private, special guest.

John was finishing the last of his coffee when the two strangers entered the dining room. He watched them cross to the back and take a seat with their backs to the wall. John had done the same, positioning himself in such a way that it

72

would be difficult for anyone to come up behind him. Old habits die hard. The pair noticed John, yet tried to show no interest.

Anyone viewing the drama may have found it amusing. Here were three grown men sizing each other up and trying not to show it. In truth, each knew the other was watching.

John placed his cup down, removed his napkin, and, with all the fortitude he could muster, rose to his feet. The back pain had subsided a little, but was still intense. He paid his tab and headed toward the stair, trying to walk as normally as he could. He did not wish to tip his hand to the strangers that he was hobbled.

All the way to his room, John's mind raced through old wanted posters. Frustration set in when he could not put names to the faces in the dining room. Was he getting too old to recall, or were these men simply unknown to him? The little voice inside would not be silenced. John could almost hear Marshal Carlson bellowing in that deep, commanding voice of his, "Boy, you got to pay attention to everything. It's the little things you miss that will get you killed!"

A misjudgment of human nature had gotten John's mentor killed. Three bandits had attacked a stagecoach on its regular run from Fort Smith to Siloam Springs near the Arkansas border with the Indian Nation. Marshal Carlson and John, along with two others, were returning to Fort

Smith with a horse thief when they heard the gunshots. Hastily, they tied the prisoner to a tree and headed to the rescue. Although the posse had arrived in time to prevent the strong box from being taken, they were too late to have stopped the robbers from killing the driver and one passenger. The perpetrators, having noticed the approaching lawmen, abandoned their objective, and lit out toward the Nation and safety from the law.

The small posse had given chase, corralling the outlaws into a narrow slot canyon. It was here Marshal Carlson made his mistake. He ordered his group around the canyon with the intention of cutting off the only other exit. He would ride alone into the canyon's main artery, intending to force the bandits into the trap.

The minor detail he had overlooked was that, sometimes a cornered animal would turn and fight. Half way down the canyon the trio of murderous desperados turned and sped back toward the canyon entrance; determined to make a stand. When John and the others heard gunfire erupt in the Marshal's direction, they raced back to aid their comrade. It was too late.

Marshal Carson's bullet-riddled body lay crumpled on the trail. John leaped from his horse and desperately checked for signs of life, but to no avail. His friend's pistols were empty and still warm. All of the wounds were in the front of his body. The old man had not gone down without a fight. Never turning his back to the oncoming danger, he had given as well as he got. But what had it mattered? The truth was the veteran man hunter of thirty years was dead due to a brief moment of not thinking through his plan.

As John opened the door to his room, his mind was still trying to place the pair downstairs. He could not recall them at all. For the present, if his back did not get better by tomorrow, he would have to find some help escorting Miller to Santa Fe. The town sheriff should know of someone willing to take the job.

John took a look at his accommodations. The feather bed was going to be way too soft for his ailing back. He had no choice but to make his bed on the floor. Sometimes a good firm surface did the trick. In the end, it probably didn't matter. Sleep tonight would be fleeting. The little voice inside was steadily becoming more difficult to put to rest.

The strangers, still enjoying a meal at Miss Sally's stuffed themselves with her cooking as they continued with tomorrow's plans.

"Where you aim to ride to in the morning?"

"Oh, I think we'll head up South Mineral Creek. I figure the gold was hidden along there somewhere. Maybe we can find it and not have to bother that old Marshal at all."

"Yeah, but it ain't likely to be found easy."

"You're probably right. If that's the case, we'll have to stick to the original plan."

"Do you really think that Miller will give up his stash?"

"I ain't ever known a man that wouldn't give up all he had to save his neck. And if he don't, then we still can get the reward for him. Either way, we win."

"Yeah, and from watching that old fart leaving a while ago, it shouldn't be any trouble to grab Miller from him."

"You know, I kind of feel sorry for him. He must really be hard up for money to try this on his own."

"Well, I'm not going to be like that in my gray years. I plan on being set."

"Yeah, or die young trying."

They finished their meal, paid the tab, left Miss Sally a generous tip, and went to their room. Morty and Willie Bee were next in line to pick up a meal to take to the prisoner.

"Miss Sally, just send the bill to the saloon and I'll get even with you," Morty said.

"Your credit is good with me Morty, just keep Willie Bee from snacking on it on the way."

"Oh, I got both eyes on him, Miss Sally. You take care."

FOURTEEN

Sheriff Keating returned to Matt's place and noticed the smell from the dead man had subsided a little. He entered without knocking and found Matt busy sewing together the heavy canvas tarps the body was carried in. Matt was skilled with delicate sutures, but the thick, curved canvas needle and heavy twine were quite the chore.

"Making him some new clothes?" quizzed the Sheriff.

"Yeah, what do you think?"

"Well, I suppose its good enough to be buried in."

"And buried he will soon be. I told the undertaker's boys to work on with lanterns and get the grave finished. I'm afraid by morning this old boy is going to be coming apart."

"You just gonna leave him in the tarps?"

"Yes sir, they won't be usable again anyway. And wrapping him up cuts the smell down a little," replied Matt. There was a soft knock at the front door.

"That's probably James from the telegraph office," said the Sheriff. "I asked him to come by and see if he knows this poor fellow."

"There isn't much to identify, but it's worth a shot," replied Matt.

James opened the door very slightly and ever so slowly.

"Doc, you in there?"

"Yes, Mr. James. Come on in," Matt answered, still sewing

the canvas.

James entered the room gingerly, as if his footsteps would wake the patient. He wasn't afraid of the dead. He'd seen plenty during his time in the War Between the States. Death was everyday and everywhere in that horrible conflict. Bodies of the young, old, and middle-aged littered battlefields from Shiloh to Gettysburg. For those four, terrible years it was as if Hell itself had opened its gates, releasing horrors on humanity the world had never before seen.

Bloated bodies were not unusual either. The retreating southern army left many gallant warriors in its wake. To James the smell of death and war was one and the same, and he hated them both. He rationalized in his mind that what General Sherman did shortened the war and, likewise, the bloodletting between North and South. The thought brought him at least some peace of mind.

"Doc, the Sheriff here thinks I might know this feller."

"I hope so, Mr. James. Now, he's been dead awhile. He doesn't he doesn't look like he did when he was alive."

Automatically James removed his hat as he approached the dead man. There was nothing to be determined by the face. Death's decay had been at work too long. Liver mortise had set in and the only thing left uncolored was the hair; shoulder length and black. James moved around the table in silence, and then stopped at the feet.

"I recognize those boots," he said, pointing with his hat.

"His boots?" asked the Sheriff, rather puzzled.

"Yep, see how that right one is walked down on the side instead of the heel."

Matt had not noticed if before. The right boot was turned out at the heel. The inside of the boot just above the heel was where the wearer placed his foot. The boot had the appearance of being very poorly made, but Matt attributed it to the deceased's having fallen arches. What was commonly called being flat-footed. The condition caused the body's weight to rest more on the insole than straight down.

"I can't say for sure it's the same feller, but them boots I know," continued James.

"I'm fairly sure it's the same guy. What can you tell me?" asked the sheriff.

"Oh, he's been coming in about once, maybe twice a month. Them boots of his always made me want to tell him to take them off and straighten them out."

"Once or twice a month," mused the sheriff. "Regular business then?"

"Not real regular," answered James. "Some months he didn't come in at all."

"Well, when he came in, what did he do?"

"He'd write out a message and I would send it."

"What kind of messages?" inquired Sheriff Keating.

"Not messages; message," answered James.
Seeing that James was taking longer than the Sheriff's patience allowed to get to the point, Matt took over the questioning.

"Mr. James, as you see, this is important. What message did he send?"

"Short one," replied James, "Your man still here."

"Your man still here?" asked the sheriff.

"Yep, that was it."

"What was the man's name?"

"He never did say."

"Well, what was this guy's name?" asked Matt, pointing to the body.

"He never said that either."

"How did he sign the message?" Sheriff Keating's irritation was increasing.

"Spotter," James shot back. "All he ever called himself was, Spotter."

"Who was the message sent to?" continued Matt.

"A fellow out in the Arizona territory; fellow by the name of John Law."

"What about this John Law?" further inquired Matt.

"Well, about a week or so after each message I would get one from Mr. Law. It was addressed to the banker here and I took it to him."

"What did the return message say?" asked the Sheriff, as he removed his hat and massaged his temples.

"It was addressed to the banker and I took it to him!" repeated James, before adding, "And there are others that sent telegraphs too."

"What others?" Sheriff Keating anxiously asked.

"Over the past four or five years there have been several that sent the same message."

"The same message?"

"Yep, except they signed them a different way. One called himself Watcher. I believe there was another one called Vulture, and one called Scarecrow. This feller, Spotter, had only been around about six months or so."

"And each one received a return message for the banker?"

"I haven't heard back from the last ones yet."

Matt picked up the telegraph receipt he had taken from the dead man's pocket. "It looks like this one was sent this past Monday. When do you expect the answer to it?"

"Oh, kinda hard to say. It's usually a couple of days," answered James. "And there was one sent Wednesday too."

"Wednesday?" questioned Matt.

"Yeah, it was a different feller, and a different message. The new feller though, still signed it Spotter. It said something about a man leaving town and going north."

The question of James was interrupted by the entrance of the three grave diggers.

"It isn't a full six foot deep, but it will do, Doctor Clark."

"Thank you boys. I'm about ready. Let's get him buried. Sheriff, you and James mind lending a hand?"

"No, at all, Doctor Matt." answered James.

The six men grabbed the canvas tarp where they could and lifted the body off the table. It was heavier than the new gravediggers expected and one of them almost lost his grip.

"Handle him easy boys," declared James, "this is the last kind deed we can ever do for him."

In silence they maneuvered the body out the back door and into Matt's wagon. There was no moon tonight, and the darkness seemed altogether fitting for the occasion. The cemetery was a short ride to the edge of town. The chosen plot was in the southeast corner where many other unnamed individuals slept in anonymity.

"Matt," spoke the Sheriff as they entered the gate, "As soon as we get him in, I'm going to go see a man."

FIFTEEN

Sheriff Keating left the cemetery and went straight to his office. Entering the front door and locking it behind him, he went out the back. The rear of the jail faced due south and in the moonless night, candles and lanterns in windows across the border could easily be seen. It wasn't yet time for his meeting, so he found a nearby barrel and sat down to wait. A voice in the dark met him.

"You early, Sheriff."

There was no mistaking the voice or the dark shape hiding in the shadows.

"I got through early and didn't want to go home. You're ahead of the clock too, my friend."

"Well, crowd small tonight. I get away sooner."

"What can you tell me about the dead man I have up here?"

"Before I tell you anything, you give me promise, okay Sheriff?"

"I don't know Padron. What promise do you want?"

"I want this hombre when you catch him."

"Padron, if I get him, he'll stand trial and be punished according to the law."

"No! I want him!"

Padron had gotten louder than he planned. He slipped back into the shadow and looked nervously in all directions.

"Padron,"continued Sheriff Keating, "I can't let you dispense vigilante justice on anyone."

"And Sheriff, you know I can no go to your court and see him punished."

"Padron, if I get this guy, and the court finds him guilty, I will drag him to one of those live oak trees on the border and hang him there. You can watch him swing from your saloon and get your revenge, but you must help me find him."

"Sheriff, is no for me; is for my Rosa."

Padron's voice broke away in tears he could not control at the mention of the name.

"Who is Rosa?"

"She is...she was...my brother's daughter. He die ten years ago. When he die he ask me to take care of her. His wife die before him and Rosa have nobody. My wife and me, we take Rosa has our own."

"You said *was* your brother's daughter., what happened to her?"

"I find her dead a week ago. Somebody kill her in a bad

way."

"Bad way?" quizzed Sheriff Keating.

"Yes…what you Americans might say, terrible way."

"Tell me about it, Padron."

Padron paused for a moment, struggling to speak through the painful memory.

"I find Rosa all tied up.....her clothes gone... and she cut all over..."

Padron had to pause for moment.

"What did you do, Padron?"

"I wrap her in sheet, take her to priest. He say the mass and bury her in church ground. Rosa always go to church, every service. She tell me she pray for me. Can you believe Sheriff, she pray for old Padron?"

Grief overwhelmed him. The sheriff remained silent as he wept through it.

"My Rosa, she was angel in this world. She no deserve this. You see Sheriff; I want this man who do this. He skin her like animal, Sheriff Keating. I want him myself!"

Without realizing it, Padron had grasped the lapels of the Sheriff's coat and was shaking them. The Sheriff waited while Padron collected himself. He had never seen him in this manner.

"Sheriff, is like I tell you, Rosa go to church all the time. She go and pray for herself and others. She say she even pray for me. You believe that Sheriff? She believe there is hope for old devil like me."

Padron stopped talking. The emotions of sorrow and hurt were at war with the ones of rage and revenge.

"Padron, tell me everything you think you know about him."

SIXTEEN

John was finishing his coffee as the sun began to make its appearance over the eastern peaks. Seldom did daybreak catch him sleeping. The street outside of Miss Sally's dining room was vacant, so it was easy to notice the two strangers readying themselves to ride out of town.

A moment of relief washed over him as he watched them prepare. Perhaps his thoughts about them were just the paranoid fears of a man who had spent his life distrusting strangers. As they passed closer to the window where he sat, the alarm returned. Their horses were not fitted for the trail. The saddlebags were missing, as were any bedrolls, and there were no canteens hanging from either pommel. These two were out for a short ride. They would be back. The silence of the moment was broken upon Willie Bee's boisterous arrival.

"Miss Sally, have you got the plate ready for that varmint down at the jail?"

"Just about, sit down and have some coffee. I'll bring it out."

Willie found the coffee pot and filled his cup. He also helped himself to some nearby cathead biscuits.

"Is the sheriff at the jailhouse?" asked John.

Willie had not noticed the Marshall and the voice startled him. It took a few seconds and some sips of coffee to clear the biscuit from his mouth so he could answer.

"Well, if it ain't that washed-up, has-been Marshal. I didn't see you sitting there." Willie was the rudest man west of the Mississippi.

" Naw, Morty is over at the saloon. I'm supposed to pick him up on my way down."

With tremendous restraint, John ignored the insult and inquired further.

"I'm done here. I'll go over there with you."

"Yeah, bring yourself on."

Miss Sally exited the kitchen with a covered dish and placed it on the counter for Willie to pick up.

"Willie, that plate is hot so watch how you grab it, and don't be snacking on it along the way."

"Oh, Miss Sally, you know me."

"Yes, I know you, so stay out of the man's breakfast."

Willie Bee took the plate as John got his hat. Both men then left out for the Outcrop. As they crossed the street, John tried to catch a glimpse of the two strangers, but they were not to be seen. He gave a quick look over the surrounding area.

To the immediate left lay the Animas River and steep mountains. The pair wouldn't have taken that route. No, they would have had to turn right, toward the end of town. That's where the South Mineral Trail started. Any rider taking this route would quickly be out of sight.

John and Willie entered the saloon to find Morty behind the bar going over the books. The sales from last night were quite a bit higher than previous Fridays. He was going to have to increase the usual Monday morning order.

"Willie Bee, you must have been pretty busy last night."

"You better believe I was, them folks was dranking faster than I could pour. Ever body was talking about that feller down there in the jail."

John was uneasy about the whole town knowing his business. He had hoped to grab his prisoner and slip out of town quietly. Even so, he was still slightly ahead of the game. He had figured on spending at least a week searching the area for the bandit. Finding him so soon put him ahead of his self-imposed schedule; even if he did still have to burn two days in town waiting for the train. With a little more luck, he would be home by Wednesday, and then he could really enjoy the rest of his days. Maybe even get to know those grown-up boys of his.

"Sheriff, how many folks in town know about this ordeal?" asked John.

"Why hell, like I said, ever body knows about it," answered Willie.

Morty looked up to see the anger building in John's face.

"Marshal, it is hard to keep a lid on something like this in a small town," explained Morty.

"It isn't too hard if folks know how to keep their mouths shut," replied John, as he stared at Willie.

"Hey, I can't help it if people want to know stuff. What am I supposed to do, just shut up and act like I don't know nothing?"

"Alright, enough of that," interrupted Morty. He then addressed the Marshal.

"Now Mister Law, I have been polite to you because of your former position, but you don't really have any authority here. Now I could keep you and that prisoner here until I check out your story with this judge you say you know, but I want that animal out of my town as soon as possible. So, I'm willing to take you at your word, but you aren't going to insult my employee."

John's anger increased at being rebuked by the part-time, small-town sheriff, but he did have to admit a new respect for Morty for defending his own. The temporary silence was broken by Willie.

"Are you two gonna stare at each other all day, or are we gonna feed that feller in the jailhouse?"

"After you, sheriff," said John as he beckoned toward the door with his hand.

D.H. Miller was awake long before the key rattled the lock in the front door of the sheriff's office. He had always been an early riser and an avid exerciser. Staying physically fit was part of his survival strategy. His thought had always been that a strong mental focus was of little value if the body could not react quickly enough when opportunity presented itself.

Morty entered first, followed by John and then Willie. They made their way, single-file, across the short walk from the door to the cell. The lawmen then took positions on each side of the room, leaving Willie between them with the breakfast plate.

Miller stood silent a few feet from the bars of his cell and carefully studied the three men. Confident the situation was still under his control; Morty went to his desk and retrieved a key. This was not the one to the cell door, but the one to a smaller door in the lower right hand corner of the bars. This opening was known as the slop door, as it was used to remove and replace the restroom facilities. Measuring only sixteen inches tall by twelve inches wide, it was also a safe place to get food to the inmates.

"Aright, now you get back against the wall and don't move," ordered Morty.

Miller obliged and Morty knelt down to open the door. He then motioned for Willie to slide the plate into the cell. Willie took two nervous steps toward the opening just as the prisoner let out a growl and lunged for the bars.

In a flurry of motion, Willie screamed, threw the plate into the air, and fled the jail before the food even hit the floor. At the same time, Morty stumbled backwards, frantically reaching for his pocket. John Law never moved. Morty regained his composure and shouted at Miller.

"Just for that, you get to go hungry!"

Miller didn't care about missing a meal. He had learned what he wanted. The fat man was not a threat, and the sheriff had hesitated before taking action. The old lawman was a different story. This man had nerve. Miller figured this man wouldn't back down from a grizzly bear.

SEVENTEEN

The two riders had kept their horses at a steady run since leaving town and were now letting them walk and catch their wind.

"Whole lot of places around here to hide a stash, you know," remarked the taller of the two.

"Yeah, I reckon that's why they never found Miller's loot," answered the other.

"I wonder if the money was ever left here in the first place."

"What other reason did he have to come back? He was safe down south, with nobody looking for him. Now, he's in jail. There is some powerful magnet that drew him up here again."

The conversation halted as the two stopped to examine an anomaly at the base of what the locals called the Clear Lake Trail.

"Looks like wagon tracks."

"Nobody is fool enough to take a wagon up that steep grade."

"Well, somebody sure is. Look at the hoof prints. Those poor animals were digging in mighty hard to get up there."

"You think that maybe someone hit the mother lode up there?"

"No, I heard that most of the mines on this side of town have played out."

"Well, maybe someone found something up there that required a wagon to haul out?"

With time to kill anyway, they decided to investigate. The trail started upwards rather abruptly and then gradually became more accessible as it wound its way up the mountain. Onward and upward, the two followed the mysterious vehicle; sharpening their tracking skills as they went.

The Stick Brothers were up early and were busy trying to determine the source of some strange noises they heard just before sunrise. Bunckus was on his belly with his head under the cabin as far as he could get it, and with both hands was trying to enlarge the opening. Gilbert knelt beside him and attempted to see under the house as well. The growling and scratching that had awakened them seemed to emanate from somewhere under the floor. Bunckus suddenly stopped digging.

"Guh...Gibbert, I chee it! Hit...hit... hit at fwyin,' bitin', tang."

"Aw, you're crazy. Get outta the way," replied Gilbert, as he pulled Bunckus aside to look for himself.

Gilbert took position at the hole and stuck his head in for a peak at the varmint.

"Dang if it ain't! I see that scannalbooger."

Gilbert pulled himself away and sat beside the cabin.

"It's him alright! He's got them teeth and stripes and his nose is turned up like this," said Gilbert, placing his index finger to his nose and turning his nostrils inside out to imitate the snarling animal.

"Et me get my tick, I, ah beat he bwain out," said Bunckus.

He quickly retrieved his weapon and proceeded to attack the badger as best he could under the floor.

The badger, for his part, had moved into what he thought would be a quiet new home just before dawn. The natural hole he had found next to the cabin wasn't quite deep enough, so the animal had taken to digging to make it bigger. This was the ruckus that had awakened the Stick Brothers, thus leading to the pitched battle between men and varmint.

The initial skirmish had been short, but explosive. The growling and biting and slashing were quite violent. And this was just on the part of the Stick Brothers. The badger, too, threw his opinion into the mix, letting the brothers know their intrusion was not appreciated.

"Gibbert, I cain't weach it," Bunckus stated.

"I tell you what, I'm gonna go around back try to poke him in the butt. When he comes out, kill him!"

"Oh, I ah I ah I beat he bwain out"

Gilbert took up his stick and was going around back to flank the badger, but stopped at the sight of the visitors.

Both boys were so preoccupied with the badger they had not noticed the riders approaching.

"Morning," greeted Gilbert.

"Morning boys," replied one of the strangers.

"What you boys doing?" quizzed the other.

"Oh, we got us a critter up under the house and we gotta get it out," answered Gilbert.

"What kind of critter?"

"I don't know but it's got teeth and claws and stripes between his eyes and his nose is turned up like he smells something that stinks."

"An, hit can fwy too," added Bunckus, who had made his way around to survey the situation.

The strangers exchanged puzzled glances. From the description, it appeared to be a badger, but the flying part just didn't fit.

"Tell us some more about this critter."

"Well, me and Bunckus," Gilbert stopped mid-sentence to make introductions.

"He's Bunckus and my name is Gilbert. Well, last week me and Bunckus was prospectin' up the mountain a ways and I fount this thang in a hole up 'ere."

"He locked onto my hand and went to bitin' and clawin' and growlin' somethin' fierce. I didn't thank I would ever get loose but, after a while he eased up to get a better bite an at's

96

when I kicked him over the cliff. And when I come down the mountain to tell Bucnkus, he said at the thang attacked him."

"Yeah, an, an, hit, ah bit me on a butt," added Bunckus.

The flying part was becoming a little more understandable, and the moment presented the strangers with too much temptation for a little mischief.

"So, you two have never seen one of these before?"

"Naw sir, we ain't from around these parts," answered Gilbert.

Leaning forward in the saddle, the shorter of the two strangers entered the conversation.

"Sounds like you boys done come across a Rocky Mountain Man-Eater."

"A man-eater," repeated the stick brothers to each other.

"Yep, and it looks like he's done tasted you two and has come back for more."

"How can at little thang eat a whole man?" inquired Gilbert.

"Oh, they don't do it all at once; you see, they just take a little bit at a time."

Playing a hunch, the rider continued, "Have you boys seen any folks around here missing a finger or a hand or maybe even a foot?"

Mining accidents were notorious for removing digits from miners, and there were a few remaining men in Silverton who had encountered such a fate.

"Yes sir," answered Gilbert, "they's one or two in town we seen that had some parts missing. There is one older feller at ain't got no foot at all. He hops around on a crutch."

"Well, there you are. See, this critter sneaks up on you in the dark and bites off a small piece just for taste. Then, if he likes you, he'll keep coming back every night for a little more. Before you know it, you'll be eaten plumb up. Yep, seems he like you boys."

Near panic, Gilbert exclaimed, "Bunckus, we gotta get this thang o-o-o-out!"

"You ah, go an poke him in a butt, an I ah, beat e bwain out."

"Now you boys go to poking it with those sticks, you're just going to make it mad."

"What can we do?" asked Gilbert.

"About the only way I know of is to smoke it out."

Trying to suppress laughter, the two decided it was time to go.

"You boys be careful. We're going to go before it gets a smell of us."

The visitors nudged their horses and headed back down the trail. Bunckus and Gilbert watched until they were out of sight, and then hurriedly proceeded to gather and stuff brush and small limbs into the hole under the cabin.

All the badger wanted was a quiet place to rest, but this was not to be. Fighting the Stick Brothers was bad enough, now his burrow was being filled with kindling. The weary animal quietly slipped away to seek a less stressful dwelling.

Returning from their fruitless venture, the two riders made their way back down the trail. Descending the pass was quicker than the climb, and in just under an hour, the riders reached Mineral Creek again.

"You don't think those two would really try to smoke that varmint out do you?"

"Come on Ab, nobody's going to build a fire under their own house."

Turning east, they spurred their horses for one last sprint before town, oblivious to the column of smoke ascending above the treetops.

EIGHTEEN

John left the telegraph office and headed for the Outcrop Saloon. He took note of the strangers returning to town. A quick glance at his watch revealed they had been gone about five hours. The time didn't mean much, but it was one of those details that John kept up with.

After sending a message home that all was well and that he should be there soon, he went to find Morty to discuss another matter. He found him sitting at a table near the door with Mister Walt.

The Saloon had a fair crowd inside. There was a low buzz of conversation and laughter. Two gents were playing billiards near the back of the room. A poker game was underway to the right of the front door. Four men were seated at the table, while others stood near watching.

Willie Bee was at his usual spot behind the bar, being his usual boisterous self. Behind him hung a magnificent beveled-edge mirror that spanned the length of the bar. It sat in a frame of carved oak and was the centerpiece of the whole room. The only flaw John noticed in the piece was that its placement revealed Willie Bee's entire backside. Morty noticed John come in and beckoned him over.

"Good afternoon Marshal. Have a seat and join us."

John took a chair facing the door, removed his hat and sat

down.

"Marshal, if you haven't already, I would like you to meet Mister Walter Murray. Mister Walt here owns and operates the King Red Mine out east of town. Mister Walt, this here is Retired U.S. Marshal, John Law from Arizona Territory."

"Mister Murray," greeted John as he extended his hand.

"Marshal, glad to make your acquaintance," returned Walt.

"Come Monday morning, the Marshall here is going to be taking our famous prisoner to Santa Fe," continued Morty.

He was speaking to Walt, but he was also reminding John that he wanted Miller out of town as soon s possible.

"Well, that's something that I want to talk about," John said, "With my back still giving me some trouble, I'm going to need some help transporting the prisoner."

"Well, I can't be leaving town. I got more to do than just look after the jail. Why, this place here takes most of my time," answered Morty. His eyes betrayed the fear he was desperately trying to suppress.

"I didn't mean you," interrupted John, "haven't you deputized anyone that would be willing to escort us to Santa Fe? The territorial court will see that they are paid."

"There isn't anybody in town that's going to take a chance of riding with that animal. Besides, who knows whether or not he's got a gang out there just a waiting to bushwhack you?" explained Morty.

John knew that Miller always traveled alone. Partners could fail and become liabilities. D.H. Miller only trusted himself.

"Sheriff, there isn't any gang!" continued John, but he never finished the sentence.

Willie Bee had been listening closely to the conversation and he could not resist the urge to join in.
"Why don't you take the Stick Brothers? They tha ones that caught him for you anyway," roared Willie.

Walt gripped his beer mug with both hands, trying to remain calm. Willie Bee always seemed to hit just the right nerve to irritate him beyond control, and he wasn't finished.

"And if ya take those two nasty thangs, you won't have to worry about no grub, cause they will eat anything."

A group of men standing at the bar took some delight in Willie Bee, and Willie loved an audience.

Leaning across the bar, he continued. "Last fall I was a deer huntin' and I came up to their cabin, and them two had done killed a porky pine; a porky pine! Why that little one was pullin' quills like he was a plucking a chicken. They asked me, did I want to join them. I told them that I wouldn't eat with them if I was starving."

"Willie, will you stay out of this? In fact, just shut up altogether," commanded Walt.

"Calm down, Mister Walt," said Morty.

"Have you ever given any thought to how much business that loud mouth might be costing you?" asked Walt.

"Some folks just don't take him as serious as you do, Mister Walt."

Walt gathered his composure and turned to John.

"I hate to say it John, but that blabber mouth might be on to something after all."

A look of amazement and fear swept across Morty's face. He could not believe the proposition that Mister Walt was about to make.

"Now, hear me out Morty," said Walt, as he continued with John.

"Those two don't have any ties here that I know of. They are good to their word, and they are two of the bravest little cusses I have ever met."

"They ain't brave; they just too stupid to be scared," added Willie.

"Willie Bee, the grown folks are talking here." Walt's temper was brewing.

"I know, and y'all keep interrupting," Willie answered back.

The group at the bar was enjoying the banter much more than Mister Walt. He picked up his beer mug and rolled it in his hands.

"Morty, what do you pay for these glasses?" asked Walt

"Oh, if I get them by the case, they are about two bits each," answered Morty.

"Well, get ready to charge me for this one," Walt angrily retorte,d.

"Now Mister Walt, just settle down. We aren't going to have any nonsense in here."

Willie couldn't leave well enough alone. He leaned again from behind the bar and made as though he were whispering; yet everyone could here.

"You know, he wouldn't be so grouchy if he would take that little old rusted pecker of his down to that whorehouse in Durango and get him a little."

Willie ducked behind the bar before he finished talking. The mug was already in flight.

The glass missed Willie Bee by about a foot, shattering against the wall only a few inches from the ornate, imported mirror. The laughter ceased and it became eerily calm, until Morty spoke up.

"Dammit, Mister Walt, that's enough of that! I think maybe it's time for you to go and cool off."

"I'm leaving. I'd rather go down to the stable and hear jackasses bray than listen that idiot another second."

Walt rose from the table, grabbed his hat, bade good-bye to John and headed for the door.

"Wait up, Mister Murray," said John, as he grabbed his hat

and followed.

Walt was still greatly irritated as he paused at the door for one last word.

"Morty, if you ever decide to get rid of that windbag, just let me know. I want to hire him. I want to take him into the deepest, darkest pit in that mine and dynamite the whole mountain down on top of him!"

Walter stormed out of the saloon with John close behind. Stopping at the edge of the wooden sidewalk to straighten his hat, he turned to make his apology to John.

"Marshal, forgive me for losing my temper, but that idiot just irritates me all over."

"No explanation needed. He gets under my skin too," replied John. "Mind if I walk a ways with you?"

"Not at all, I'm just heading back to the mine," answered Walt.

"What about these Stick Brothers?" queried John.

Walt paused for a moment and began to slightly chuckle.

"Well, Bunckus and Gilbert first showed up here about a year ago. They came to the assay office with a small amount of ore and were trying to sell it when I first met them."

"Are they miners?" asked John.

"No, they were just looking for someone to buy a small amount of gold that they had worked out of the mountains. It wasn't enough to be worthwhile, so I bought it and added it to my daily milling. I think the total was about eight dollars."

"Eight dollars," repeated John.

"Yes, and since then I have bought a little more from them. Last fall they brought in some twenty five dollars worth."

"Not much for a season's work."

"No sir and they spent nearly fifteen dollars of that on hay and grain to get their horses through the winter," continued Walt.

"Why don't they give up and try making a living somewhere else?" asked John.

"The boys say they got to pay off a marker. Now, I don't know how much they owe or to whom they owe it, but he must be one hard-nosed lender. They shoveled manure out of the livery stable for a solid day for fifty cents apiece," continued Walt.

"Pitiful wages for such a dirty job," said John.

"Ben didn't mean to slight them. He said it was all he could afford, and Bunckus and Gilbert took the job. They told him the same story about needing the money for that marker," replied Walt.

"So, you think they will agree to escort a prisoner?"

"Marshal, for a day's wage, they will hand carry him to Santa Fe."

John removed his hat and massaged the back of his neck.

Fatigue was beginning to settle in. He was not completely comfortable with the plan running through his mind, but there did not seem to be much choice. He reminded himself that within forty-eight hours this should be ended. He would be in Santa Fe Monday night and the prisoner would be someone else's problem.

"If I was of a mind to, where would I find these guys?" asked John.

"Now Marshal, you need to think on this real hard before you do anything. Those two boys are not...well, there not...ah...you just need to meet them before you decide."

"You know yourself, Mr. Murray that since Willie Bee has told everybody within earshot who this prisoner is and what he is suspected of doing, I am not going to get any help in this town. Now, I don't foresee any trouble getting the prisoner delivered; I just want some assistance in case he gets unruly. So where can I find them?"

"They live in an old abandoned shack about two hours ride east of town.

Pointing to the south, Walter continued, "You take Main Street here until the city limits and then...I tell you what, I'll take you up there tomorrow."

"I don't want to put you out Mister Murray," responded John.

"Oh, it's no bother. I could use a little quiet time. And,

by the way, it's Walter."

"Fair enough, folks call me John."

"It's settled then, John. I'll see you in the morning. How about 6:00?"

"Sounds good, where you want to meet?" asked John.

Walt was a little surprised by the question. He had forgotten that John was not a local and didn't know that Miss Sally's was the only morning place to be.

"I will meet you at Miss Sally's place. She has the best eye opening coffee around," answered Walt.

"Until then," replied John.

The two men shook hands and parted company. Walt crossed the street and made his way toward the mine. He gave some thought to stopping by Dr. Edmund's office along the way. He and Doctor Edmund were about the same age and shared many like interests. After the ordeal with Willie Bee some intelligent conversation might just lower his blood pressure. Meanwhile, John headed to the livery stable to make arrangements for a horse for tomorrow's ride. He then paid a visit to Hal and ordered a pair of shackles to be made for his prisoner. Hal said he could do it for about two dollars. He laughed and said he was giving John a discount because he liked putting chains on "white folks."

John laughed with him and agreed on the price.

NINETEEN

Right on time, John and Walt met at Miss Sally's for breakfast. John noticed the strangers were not present. He pondered the thought that maybe they had left town early, but this idea was soon put to rest as the duo entered the dining room. With a quick glance in his direction, they took seats against the back wall where they could easily watch entrances and exits.

Since it was a Sunday morning and early, the room was nearly empty. Miss Sally was as cheerful as ever. She waited on John and Walt herself.

"Mr. Law, is your back any better?" she asked.

"Yes ma'am. It eased up some last night."

"Mr. Walt, you don't normally come in at this hour…and on a Sunday too! What are you two fixing to get into?"

"Now, Miss Sally, you know all three of us have done got too old to get into much of anything."

"You speak for yourself, Mr. Walt. I'm not dead yet," she replied with a chuckle.

"Miss Sally," responded John, "I asked Walt here to take me out to where those two boys, Gilbert and Bunckus, live."

"Oh those two dear young uns, I wish folks in town

wouldn't treat them so mean. I know they get into things, but I don't think they mean no harm to nobody."

"Marshal, you aren't going out to cause any trouble, are you?"

"Oh no, Miss Sally, I'm thinking of asking them to help me with a project. Walt says they are eager and willing to work."

"They don't shy away from working. I use 'em whenever I can. No sir, they don't mind working."

"Well, maybe we can help each other then," answered John.

Breakfast and conversation lingered on. There didn't seem to be any reason to hurry. It was nearly seven o'clock before the two men finished and rose to leave.

The two strangers lingered also. They were very interested in why John and Walt were together. Their curiosity was further heightened when they saw the two men leave together.

"What do you suppose they are up to?" asked the taller of the pair.

"I can't quite figure. Give them about half a minute and we will follow.

There was no need to follow; the answer waited just

outside the window. Walt led John to a pair of horses, saddled and tied to the hitching post.

"I didn't know you were providing horses, Walt."

"I'm sorry, I thought I told you. I only have these two. When I was child, my dad and I raised and trained horses for hunting. I still enjoy fooling with them."

"I made arrangements with Ben to rent one. Let me go by and tell him I don't need it and we will be off."

"You want to go by the jail and check on your prisoner before we leave?"

"I done that last night and again before I came here. He's still secure."

"Man, don't you ever sleep?"

"Only with one eye closed," John answered with a grin, as he climbed into the saddle.

The strangers watched John and Walt ride down the street to the livery. They watched the stable owner become very animated on their arrival. He waved his hands, shook his head, and pointed several times to a third horse that was saddled and ready for the trail.

They exchanged questioned looks at each other as they watched the men leave the livery and head back toward them. John and Walt slowly passed Miss Sally's and rode on out of town, taking the South Mineral Trail to the west. The same direction the two strangers had traveled yesterday.

"Why would an old law man take an old banker out for a ride this early in the morning?" asked the taller one.

"Yeah, and into an area where gold coin is rumored to be hidden," answered the shorter one.

"Let's get saddled and follow."

"No, too easy to be spotted on that narrow road; let's wait and see what they bring back."

TWENTY

John and Walt followed the well-worn trail out of town and into the mountains. John instinctively studied the ground for signs, noticing the different tracks and directions they took. Walt surveyed the scenery all around. The landscape still brought a special kind of awe to him.

The sights and sounds never grew old. A hawk circled overhead. Watchful chipmunks peered out of their burrows. The gurgling creek meandered its way without noticing either.

Walt was about to tell John to take the narrower trail to their right, but he noticed he had already turned and was headed up it. Without realizing it, John left the main route and began following a smaller one. He had noticed the tracks of a pair of horses that had recently traveled this way.

"I didn't think you knew where the cabin was," stated Walt.

"Oh, I don't. Sorry, I was just checking out these prints. Looks like a couple of folks have been this way not too long ago."

"This trail switchbacks up the mountain to Clear Lake. There are a few abandoned mines along the way. I think the old bridge is still passable, but it isn't used much these days, except for sightseers. The cabin is about halfway up."

They slowly snaked their way up the trail. John kept looking for a campsite. There was a slight smell of smoke from time to time, but he didn't see any sign of fire.

"Mr. Walt, I smell something burning."

"Me too, not real often, but every now and then I catch a bit of a whiff of smoke."

"Folks camp around here?"

"Oh yeah, and when summer gets on, there will be quite a few folks in this area."

Silence resumed as the two men zigzagged their way up the mountain. In a little over an hour they reached to source of the smoke that had been wafting across the area. There was a clearing off to the left, and the smoldering ashes of what used to be a cabin. On the edge of the clearing stood a wagon with a horse harnessed to it and another tied behind.

John immediately returned to his lawman character. He pulled the horse to a halt and grabbed Walt's arm to stop him. The little voice within was issuing commands to check for potential danger. It was also chastising him for not bringing his guns.

Surveillance of the clearing was abruptly ended when two weary heads poked above the wooden sides of the wagon. The boys were a sight to behold. They had tried to put the fire out, but were obviously unsuccessful. The old wood of their former home went up like paper once the fire got started.

After the flames died down, the boys dug through the ashes looking for the carcass of the badger. Both were covered in soot. Since they did not find it, they were convinced it was still nearby waiting for them to go to sleep. They spent the night awake in the wagon, jumping at every noise.

Bunckus had been crying, and his attempts to wipe the tears smeared the soot on his face into a garish mask. He sort of resembled a raccoon in reverse.

"Gilbert, Bunckus…you boys alright?" questioned Walt.

"Yes sir. We just had a far." answered Gilbert.

Walt rode on into the clearing. He did not share John's concern about danger lurking everywhere.

"I'll say you had a fire. What happened?"

"We was tryin' to smoke this Rocky Mountain Man-Eater out from under the house, an...."

"Hit poof!" interjected Bunckus.

"You built a fire under the house?" asked Walt.

"Well, at's where this thang was," answered Gilbert.

Walt raised his hand to halt the conversation when John rode up and joined the trio.

"Boys, this is John Law. He is a U.S. Marshal, and…"

Bunckus and Gilbert exchanged a terrorized glance with each other and drew closer together.

"Just settle down. You boys aren't in trouble. Now, what was under the house?"

"They said it was ah Rocky Mountain Man-Eater…"

"Wait, who said?"

"We don't know. They just came ridin' up while we was tryin' to poke it out from under the house."

The lawman in John kicked in when he heard about two unknowns riding up.

"Start at the top. How did this get started?"

"Well, Bunckus heard something scratchin' and growlin' under the floor yesterday morning. He thought it might be a bear. I told him a bear couldn't fit under the house, but he had to go look."

John and Walt looked intently as Gilbert continued.

"We got outside and sure 'nuff, somethin' had done dug up under the house. Bunckus poked his head in the hole it dug and when he did, he screamed and jumped about five

116

feet backards…said it was that flyin', bitin' thang."

"A what?" asked Walt.

"Well, Mr. Walt, me and Bunckus was prospecting a couple days ago. I was huntin' in this hole and this thang grabbed me. It durn near eat my hand plumb off. You can still see the marks." Gilbert showed them his scratched hands.

"You mean a burrowing owl or something like it?" Walt inquired again.

"No sir, it ain't no bird. It ain't got no feathers. It's all furry, with claws and teeth. And it's got stripes down its head and it sticks it nose up like it smells something at stinks."

"An an an hit, hit can fwy too!" added Bunckus.

John regretted asking for the full story. "Never mind about that, what about the two men you say rode up here?"

"Well, we was busy tryin' to poke this thang out from under the floor. We didn't see 'em ridin up, they was just there. They asked us what we was doin'. When we told 'em about this thang, they said it was a Rocky Mountain Man Eater. They said the only way to git it out was to smoke it out."

"An an an we ah we ah ah twied, but hit hit ah poof!"

John did not have any problem believing the old cabin

would go up in flames fairly quick. It was little more than dried kindling anyway. What he had difficulty grasping was anyone setting a fire under it but, behind them, in a smoldering heap, lay the evidence.

"What about the men? Can you describe them?"

"Well, they was dressed real fine. They had two ah the purdiest horses we ever seen."

There was no doubt the strangers in town were the ones in question. Walt stepped in to change the subject back to the reason for their visit.

"Boys, like I said earlier, John here is a U.S. Marshal. Now, he would like to hire you two for a couple of days to help with a prisoner."

"I will pay you boys two dollars a day, plus room and board. I'll also furnish the train tickets both ways. I figure it will take about two days; three at the most. In fact, I'll pay you for three days no matter," promised John.

The Stick Brothers looked at each for a moment. They were both thinking the same thing. Twelve dollars was more than they had made in a long time. It sure as heck beat fifty cents for shoveling manure. Gilbert and Bunckus exchanged a quick glance with each other and agreed.

"Yes sir, we will help you. Where is this prisoner and

where we takin' him?" asked Gilbert.

"He's in the jail in Silverton. We're going to take him to Santa Fe. I plan to leave tomorrow on the train."

"Is he at feller you and Mr. Morty locked up the other day?"

"That's him," John answered, but was quickly interrupted by Bunckus.

"At cookie 'tomper! I ain't goin, I ain't goin, I ain't...."

"Hush, Bunckus," scolded Gilbert.

"I ain't. At tump a bit 'tomped my cookie. I ain't going, I ain't, I ain't, I ain,t." The madder Bunckus became, the less he seemed to stutter.

"Bunckus, quit actin' ignert," scorned Gilbert.

"I ain't actin'."

Gilbert cupped Bunckus's face between his hands to calm him down and to also look directly into his eyes.

"Now Bunckus, we done told the Marshal we would do it. We can use tha money for at marker, and asides, we ain't got no house no more."

Bunckus surveyed the pile of ashes and soot that used to be a cabin. He remembered they did not find evidence of the badger in the rubble, so he settled down and agreed to go.

119

"So, it's a deal then," proclaimed Walt.

"It's a deal on my end," agreed John. "You boys come on to town today. I'll set you up at Miss Sally's so we can leave as soon as the train is ready."

"Oh, wees ready now," said Gilbert.

John and Walt waited while Gilbert and Bunckus took the lead, he thought it strange that they had two horses, but only a single tree hook-up for the wagon. The other horse was tethered behind. It wasn't long until the quartet was moving down the mountain toward town.

TWENTY ONE

D.H. Miller completed his morning physical exercises and was sitting on his bunk working through some mental ones. He thought it vital to stay fit in body and mind so that he could grasp an opportunity when it arrived and be able to act upon it. Keeping his mind busy also kept the panic attacks at bay. The claustrophobia of confinement amplified their frequency and severity. Space was limited in the cell for a workout, but he managed.

The cramped quarters also offered very little in the way of mental stimulation. He had already counted the number of floor planks from his cell to the jail door. Taking the total and multiplying it by four inches, he estimated the distance to be about twenty four feet. This distance he then divided into the strides of an average man, and figured to be to about eight This convinced him that it was too much open space to have to cross if he tried to push past one of his keepers and run for it.

D.H. had also counted the number of stones in each of the four walls of the jail. He compared the difference of the largest stone to the smallest and worked out what he thought was a fair estimate of the average weight of each stone. With this he multiplied it by the total of stones and determined a weight for the materials.

In addition to his calculations, Miller also listened. He had been only semi-conscious when they brought him in, so he wasn't really sure where the jail was in relation to the rest of the town. But he knew that sounds can convey information where sight is limited.

Most of the town's noise came from the right of the jail. The previous evening being a Saturday, the activity from that side had been especially boisterous. The faints sounds of a piano, mixed with the laughter of intoxication led him to conclude that the saloons were down that direction. Sounds coming from the left appeared suddenly, and traffic going that direction ended equally as sudden. Miller came to the assumption that the jail must be located near the end of the town. If given an occasion to flee, that would be the preferred direction to take.

His mental layout of Silverton was actually quite accurate, just based upon interpreting its noise. But, this morning D.H. was pondering another mental puzzle. Why had the Marshal come so early? Why the change of routine? Were they planning on moving him today?

His thoughts were interrupted by the unlocking of the door. It opened all the way before Morty slowly stepped inside. The sheriff had developed a fear of Miller getting out of the cell and pouncing on him as soon as he came through the door. D.H. found this amusing.

The person following Morty into the jail got the prisoner's attention. It wasn't Willie Bee or the Marshal. It was an elderly lady carrying a covered tray.

Willie Bee, as usual, was far too hung over to be up yet. His duties at the Outcrop weren't only confined to serving drinks; he also cleaned up the place after closing. Any liquor left in the glasses, he would pour into a quart jar he kept on a shelf under the bar. The mix was beyond description and never the same, but the alcohol content was high and free.

Last night's leftovers nearly filled Willie bee's jar. He, however, made sure it was empty before morning. The concoction had been potent. His eyes likely wouldn't see the light of day for several hours yet.

"Set the tray on my desk, Miss Sally. I'll pass it to him when the Marshal gets back," said Morty, gesturing with his hand toward his desk.

"Now Morty, it will get cold. Ain't no telling when he and Mr. Walt will return."

"That doesn't matter. You aren't going near that cell."

Miss Sally was about to further protest when D.H. spoke up.

"It's alright ma'am. It will be fine."

Morty was somewhat taken aback by the voice. Except for the growl on the first day, he had not heard a sound from the prisoner. Miller was equally surprised by his comments. He had not meant to. It came before he could stop it. This was a sign of weakness to him; a sign of caring. Internally he chastised himself, yet was determined not to show any outward emotion. A huge panic attack was approaching. He had to get control.

Miss Sally said nothing in response. Setting the tray down on the heavy, wooden desk, she quietly left. Morty followed close behind, locking the door as he went.

Alone again, D.H. began to gather himself by analyzing what was said about the Marshal being gone. Where had he gone and who was this Mr. Walt he had taken with him? Were there more deputies to deal with? His plans were based on the Marshal's having too much pride to ask for help. Had he guessed wrong?

"Nonsense!" he said to himself, slowly gaining his composure.

No one could outmaneuver him. This was just a minor setback. He would work through the difficulties. Manipulating people was something he was very good at. It was just a matter of watching and reading them. He already had learned that Willie Bee and Morty were too timid to be of any use. The Marshal had too much pride in himself to try to coerce. Miss Sally though, she had compassion. A dangerous flaw he could exploit.

TWENTY TWO

The Lady of Guadalupe mission had gone through many changes in its two hundred fifty year history. Somehow, though, the old mission seemed as timeless as ever. Its white, stucco walls and familiar arches were as much a part of the landscape as the sagebrush, cactus, and sand from which it sprang. The bell tower was a dominant feature of the structure, supporting the bell and the cross in front and looming high above the main building. An iron fence surrounded the perimeter of the courtyard, as well as the cemetery.

Two rows of trees flanked the front and west side of the tower. They offered welcomed shade to parishioners entering and exiting the sanctuary. A row of wooden tables with benches were lined up in the shadow of these trees. This made a natural spot for outdoor gatherings. At times the church members shared a meal and conversation here. There was never any gossip, of course, just commentary on community activities. The church and its accompanying buildings stood out against the surrounding desert. Yet, at the same time, they seemed as natural a part of the landscape there as much as the native scrub and cactus did.

Padron was standing in the shadow of one of the more distant trees. He was not interested in the usual Sunday comments of those exiting the services this morning. The inner workings of the church were of no real concern to him. He was familiar with the order of service. As a young boy, his parents forced him and his brother to attend. He remembered how old Father Pena had been determined to make altar boys of them.

But, Padron wanted no part of that. He had different plans. At the age of thirteen, he ran away from home, church and all things spiritual. He tried his hand at cattle wrangling, sheep herding, and even driving freight wagons. By the time he was sixteen, he realized these involved great effort, but yielded little pay.

He had always been a large child for his age and his stocky build caught the attention of one of the border town saloon owners. He hired Padron to be his bouncer at a day's wage that far exceeded what he had found thus far. The rest, they say, is history. By the time he was twenty, he had his own business. It was a moneymaker from the start, and Padron learned quickly how to make the underside of society even more lucrative. The more he went down the dark path though, the less he heard the church bells. It had been nearly four decades since he'd noticed them at all.

Then Rosa had dropped into his life. Padron and his wife never had children. Rosa's mother had died of influenza when the little girl was only six. Two years later, her father was killed in a railroad accident. The only family she had left was Padron and his wife. Following her father's funeral, this was the natural place for her to go. She had won the hearts of both of them from the start.

For the past ten years she had been the center of their life. But that was all gone now. Rosa was all gone now. Padron and his wife were left with only bittersweet memories.

Rosa was the reason for Padron's visit to the church today. Father Montoya exited the building behind everyone else. Looking across the yard, he noticed Padron. With a stern and surprised look he approached.

"Francisco, you come to visit Rosa again?" inquired Father Montoya.

Practically everyone knew him as just Padron, but the name by which he had been baptized was, Juan Francisco de Campos. Very few were allowed to call him Francisco. He responded to the priest.

"I visited Rosa this morning, Padre. It is you I would like to talk to, if you have time."

Padron had a fair command of the English language due his business location. It was always refreshing, though, to converse his native tongue.

"You may have all my time you need, my son."

The priest motioned with his hand toward a nearby table with a pair of benches; one on each side. The two sat down, each choosing a spot opposite the other. There was a moment of silence before any conversation began. Padron started it off.

"Padre, you stand in front of your church and tell the people about a loving God who is to be trusted and obeyed. A God, who sees all, knows all, a God who is all powerful. Is this not so, Padre?"

Padron was trying to keep his composure, but with great difficulty. Father Montoya said a rapid and silent prayer before answering.

"Yes, Francisco, I do."

"And do you believe this, Padre?"

The priest made another quick and silent prayer.

"Yes, I most certainly do, my son."

"Then tell me, man of God, where was this God when my Rosa was murdered? She believed in your God. She prayed to your God. She trusted your God. Tell me, Padre, where was this God when my Rosa was tortured to death?"

The priest pondered the question. It came up often. This was not the first time the age-old quandary of suffering, pain, and evil in the world had been presented to him. He weighed his answer very carefully. Father Montoya had performed the last rites for Rosa. He saw the condition of her body, and still had problems sleeping some nights.

"My son, evil exists. It does not mean that God doesn't. God gives all of us free will. Some choose evil."

"That is not an answer. If God cannot control evil, then He is not all-powerful. If He doesn't see it in time to stop it, then He is not all-knowing. If He sees it and doesn't stop it, then He cannot be all-loving. No, Padre, your God does not exist, and you should stop lying to people." Padron fought desperately to remain calm, but hurt and anger were winning the battle.

The priest took his time to speak. He knew his response was critical to the conversation.

"Francisco, do you want to live in a world run by a God who controls everything you do? I understand you left the church many years ago. God let you leave. God let you choose your own path. Even though that path may not have been the one He chose for you, He let you choose it. What if God had stopped you as you were leaving the church? Would you choose that kind of God? Would you serve that kind of God? My son, God gives each of us free will so that, when we stand in judgment, if we are condemned, it will be of our own choosing."

Padron was silent for a moment. The thought of judgment bothered him.

"Then tell me, why would God let an innocent, young girl die, while letting an old devil like me live to old age?"

"Maybe God knows you are not ready for the judgment, and because He loves you, He is giving you time to get ready."

The priest's words sank into Padron's heart like a flaming arrow. He almost clutched his chest in response. The image of standing before the throne of God terrified him. The thought of being cast away into eternal damnation was unsettling. For a man who did not believe in hell, it sure felt real now. Father Montoya continued.

"Where do you see Rosa now? Is she gone forever? Is she now nothing more than a dead, cold body in a dark grave? Or can you see her in the presence of her Lord; safe from any harm for all eternity? Can you picture her maybe even waiting for you?"

The words were driving the arrow deeper into Padron's heart.

"Dreaming something doesn't make it real, Padre."

"My son, I cannot prove to you that God exists. Likewise,

you cannot prove that He doesn't. We must look honestly at the evidence before us and believe accordingly. So, tell me Francisco, where do you believe Rosa is now?"

Silence resumed for a moment. Then Padron spoke.

"Padre, forgive me for calling you a liar. You really believe what you preach. I think you are a fool, but you are not a liar. I must go now."

"I will pray for you, Francisco."

"It would be better to spend that time on someone who can benefit from it."

Father Montoya was not ready to end the meeting, but he sensed Padron was. He carefully presented his last query.

"If you don't believe God exists, then who are you angry with, Francisco?"

Padron picked up his hat and left. He had no answer for the last question.

TWENTY THREE

It was early afternoon when John, Walt, and the Stick Brothers made their way back into town. They stopped in front of Miss Sally's.

"Walt, give me a few minutes to square these boys away with a room, then I'll go with you and help tend to the horses."

"No need for that John. You take care of this. I got the horses. One of those things I sort of like tending to myself. No offense intended."

"No offense. I greatly appreciate all of your help. See you for supper?"

"Just might, just might."

John dismounted and handed the reins to Walt. Walt took them, but before leaving gave a final admonition to Bunckus and Gilbert.

"You boys try to behave and don't make me regret introducing you to the Marshal."

The boys promised and Walt nudged his horse towards home, leading the other behind. John started into Miss Sally's, but he noticed the boys did not follow.

"Are you two coming?"

Bunckus and Gilbert exchanged awkward glances with each other. They were not sure if they could explain to John their reluctance.

"Marshal John, maybe we could just stay at tha livery with Mr. Ben. We gotta take tha horses and wagon down anyways."

John noticed the boy's appearance again. They were quite a sight. The worn and tattered clothes must have been embarrassing on their own. The layer of black soot must have only added to the shame.

The Marshal quickly realized though, that it was more than just their appearance. These two young men were broken on the inside. He thought back on all the comments he had heard about the "Stick Brothers". The detractors had not been quiet in their derisions. Bunckus and Gilbert knew how the town felt about them.

Feelings of compassion began to stir in John. He agreed to let the boys take their horses and wagon to the livery, but he was not going to let them sleep there.

"You boys go square your animals with Ben. Tell him you'll be back for them in a couple of days. I'm going in and set things up with Miss Sally. Meet me at the back door when you get through. You can wash up a bit before you come inside."

Bunckus and Gilbert were still uncomfortable.

"Well, Marshal John, ain't no need spending money fer a room. We can stay with Mr. Ben..."

"No," said John, firmly. Now you boys do as I said." John tried to ease the situation with a bit of levity.

"Besides, I'm not going to ride the train beside you two like that."

"Yes sir," responded Gilbert. "We'll be right back."

The boys started off to the livery and John went in to see Miss Sally. The whole scene had been carefully observed by the two strangers. They were strategically seated in the dining room with a clear view of the front door and as much of the main street as the windows would allow.

"Looks like the lawman and his banker got back," said the taller of the two.

"Yeah and they picked up those two we met yesterday. But, did you get a look at them?"

"They've been roughed up alright."

"You think maybe the lawman and his banker had to persuade them to tell something?"

"I don't know. I'm going to stroll on out and see where

they take the wagon. You hang back and learn what you can here."

The shorter of the pair nodded slightly and leaned his chair against the wall while his partner slipped out the front door.

John was at the front desk waiting for Miss Sally to finish something in the kitchen. The strangers thought their actions went unnoticed, but John missed very little. He was certain they were not D.H. Miller's partners. Miller always traveled and worked alone. They were not regular tourists either. It figured to him that they must be bounty hunters.

There was, after all, a substantial reward for Miller's capture. The area was also filled with constant rumors of the gold from the Ophir robbery still lying around somewhere just waiting to be found. But, if they had been bounty hunters, why had they not left once Miller had been apprehended and jailed? Also, how had they heard of the outlaw's location in Silverton?

Miss Sally came out of the kitchen. She was red-faced from leaning over the cook stove, and her hair was a bit unkempt from her wiping sweat from her brow with her forearms. She smiled when she saw John.

"John, you and Walt enjoy your ride?"

"It was alright, Miss Sally."

She looked beyond him and scanned the dining room for Mr. Walt.

"You by yourself?" she quizzed.

"Not exactly, Walt will be back later, but I got two more I need you to fix up. They'll need a room for tonight, and they need a bath in the worst kind of way."

John explained the ordeal Bunckus and Gilbert had been through. He also told of his plan to have them escort Miller to Santa Fe. Miss Sally's expression turned to sorrow and sympathy upon hearing the news. Tears were forming.

"Oh, and they could use some clothes. All they got is what they're wearing and it's not much. Is there any place to get them something to wear?"

"I think I can find them something…and I'll get a tub of hot water ready. You go get them and tell them to meet me around back."

Miss Sally returned to the kitchen to start everything for the boys. John noticed she was wiping her face with her apron. The tears could no longer be contained.

"Marshal, it's about time you got back," interrupted Morty. I need you to help feed your prisoner."

Without answering, John turned and followed the Sheriff

out the door.

A few minutes later, Bunckus and Gilbert arrived at Miss Sally's back door. There was a nice meal ready for them. She said it was leftovers from the lunch crowd, but the food was fresh and still sizzling hot.

"You boys sit and eat while the bath water is heating up. I got some errands to run, but I'll be back in a little bit."

TWENTY FOUR

Sheriff Keating sat in his office leaning back with his eyes closed. He was trying to unravel and make sense of the previous day. His Sunday afternoon reflections were interrupted by Dr. Clark's entrance.

"Sleeping your life away Sheriff," Matt said in jest.

"I'm awake. I'm just trying to figure some of this mystery out," replied the Sheriff.

"It is a mystery at that," said Matt. "We have a stranger found dead in a water trough, more strangers watching another stranger, who appears to have left town, and then another stranger pretending to be one of the other strangers and signing his name to the last telegraph."

"There is another mystery, Matt," added Sheriff Keating.

"Oh?"

"Yep, there's another death; a girl, south of the border."

Sheriff Keating explained as best he could about Rosa and Padron without naming names.

"When was the girl killed?" asked Matt.

"Best I can figure, just a day or so before our first stranger met the water trough."

Matt pondered the new revelation.

"Matt, do you still think the man in the water trough was tortured for information?"

"Well, it would fit that the girl was done in for the same reason…information," said Matt. "You say she was skinned?"

"Yes, and left to be found…just like the water trough man. No attempt to hide her."

"This guy not only wanted information, he enjoyed inflicting the pain and terror," added the Dr.

"Well Matt, I have to find him. He may still be here. That last telegram could have been a ruse."

"Oh, I think he's gone alright, Sheriff. Look at this."

Matt produced a tiny nugget of gold from his vest pocket and placed it in Sheriff Keating's palm. With a puzzled expression, the Sheriff looked at the nugget and then to Matt.

"How does a gold nugget suggest he's gone?"

"Look closely Sheriff, that's not a nugget. It's a chipping from a gold bar. See the straight rounded edge? I know it's tiny, but that shape is manmade. It is not natural."

"Alright, it's a piece from a gold bar. What of it?"

"Look closer. Do you see the 'D' stamped on it?"

Albert walked to the window for more light and carefully examined the specimen up close. It was small, but once you saw it, it was plain. The letter "D" was stamped on the edge of the piece.

"Matt, I got enough to try to figure out as it is. Explain your theory," demanded the Sheriff.

"Sheriff, I think that's a piece of a gold bar from the Denver Mint," answered Matt.

"Okay and what of it?"

"Well if it is, then it's proof that it's from a bar and not a coin, because Denver doesn't mint coins. About ten years ago, a couple of brothers named Clark, no kin of mine, partnered with a Mr. Gruber to form a private mint in Denver. They minted gold coins for about three years, and then the Federal Government bought them out. The government has yet to make any coins. They only mint gold bars. They take local gold, melt it, form it into bars, weigh it, stamp it, and return it to the depositors."

Albert was listening, but he wasn't connecting any of the dots.

Matt continued. "If this is from the Denver mint, then it is local gold that was minted and returned to its owners."

"Okay. It's from a bar of privately-owned gold mined

somewhere near Denver. What of it?"

"Sheriff, about five years ago a shipment of gold was hijacked on a return trip from the Denver mint. It had been sent from the Ophir mine. The teams and drivers were found dead on the road between Ouray and Ophir. The bullion was gone and never recovered."

"Go on," urged the Sheriff. He was interested now.

"The story goes that the shipment was worth about eighty thousand dollars. The standard gold bar is about four hundred ounces…around twenty five pounds. This would come out to ten of these bars. It would be hard to escape with two hundred fifty pounds of gold, but a single bar could be made off with. The rest could have been hidden and recovered later."

"And how do you know all this?"

"I have some of the bigger city newspapers mailed to me down here. The news is sometimes a few weeks old, but they keep me kind of informed"

"So you think our mystery man has gone back for the rest?"

"Not really. I don't think money is all that important to this guy."

"Why do you say that?" questioned Sheriff Keating.

"Well," continued Matt, "at today's gold price, a single bar is worth around eight thousand dollars. If he spent that much around here in the last few years, somebody would have noticed. This guy has been very careful not to be noticed.

"Maybe has hasn't been here that long. Maybe he didn't get a whole bar of gold to start with," added the Sheriff.

"I think he had a whole bar. No need to spend time breaking it up right away…just stuff one in a saddle bag and ride off. I don't think he had any partners either, or if he did, they were silenced."

"How do figure that?"

"No one was ever apprehended for the robbery. This much money would have come into circulation by now. It would be nearly impossible to keep everyone quiet about it."

"Alright, but if our man is part of the Ophir robbery and murders, why do you think he's been here since then? And where did you get this piece of gold?"

"Those two questions have a single answer," replied Matt.

"Well, let's hear it."

"The dry goods store."

Albert and Matt were fairly close friends. The two men worked together quite well on occasions, but they were worlds apart in personality. Albert liked things short and direct. He asked direct questions and wanted direct answers. When he was questioning a suspect, he had little patience for their long, drawn-out answers given while trying to avoid guilt.

Matt, on the other hand, enjoyed the story. He wanted people to hear more than just his conclusions; he wanted them to understand his reasoning for them.

"Matt, will you get to the point? Am I going have to put you in a water trough?"

"Mr. Klein came to see me this morning with a broken arm. He said he fell while stocking his top self. It wasn't a bad break, so I set it and put a plaster on it. He asked what he owed and when I told him, he paid me with this. I questioned him about it and he said a fellow had been coming in every now and then for about the past four years and buying supplies with pieces just like it."

The Sheriff was definitely interested now.

"Matthew, let's go see Mr. Klein."

TWENTY FIVE

The sun was about an hour from sinking behind the western ridges before Bunckus and Gilbert had finished bathing and dressing. John was surprised at how much change a little soap and a lot of scrubbing could accomplish.

"You boys look totally different."

"Yes sir, Miss Sally got us eaze clothes," answered Gilbert.

"They are very nice."

Before John could continue, Miss Sally joined in.

"Oh, they're just some things my late husband never wore. I figured the boys might as well get some use out of them."

Miss Sally was telling the truth about her late husband and the clothes. In all honesty he had never worn them. One reason was that they were not his size. The other reason was because she had just bought them. While the boys were taking their baths, she had persuaded the owner of the local general store to open up on this Sunday afternoon.

"Let's get you two settled in a room," continued John. "We got a big day tomorrow."

He turned to go, but looking back, noticed Gilbert was fixated on the small room at the end of the hall. It was about five feet square with a small vanity on the wall to the left of the door. A white, porcelain bowl sat snugly against the back wall. This bowl resembled a chair, but the top was open and seemed to have water in it. There was a pipe leading from the back of this bowl chair that connected to a tank on the wall above it. A brass chain dangled from the bottom of the wall tank. The chain reached to within a few feet of the bowl and ended in small brass handle. Anyone seated on the bowl could reach and pull the chain if he so desired.

While Bunckus had been busy finishing his bath and getting dressed, Gilbert had been watching folks enter and exit this room. They went in one at a time, and closed the door behind them. After a few minutes there would be a gurgling, flushing sound, and then they would exit.

"Marshal John, what is at room fer?"

John was genuinely perplexed by the question, yet the expression on Gilbert's face told him the man was serious.

"It's called a water closet or, as some folks call it, a crapper…it's a bathroom."

Gilbert again examined the small bowl.

"Ats a mighty small bathtub. Is it just fer washing ya hands and feet?"

"No," responded John. "You know what an outhouse is, don't you?"

"Yes sir, of course."

"Well, that's an indoor outhouse."

"You mean they take a dump inside the house?"

"That's one way of putting it, I guess."

Gilbert exchanged a look of disgust and disbelief with Bunckus.

"You know, Bunckus, some folks is just plain nasty."

John was not in a mood for further educating these two. He turned and led the way upstairs.

The strangers were back in the dining room as John and the "Stick Brothers" went upstairs.

"So, you say the wagon was empty?" asked the shorter .

"Yep, only thing in there is an old butter churn stuffed with papers."

"And you say the livery manager confirmed that the Marshal has hired those two for deputies to escort Miller to Santa Fe?"

"Yep. That loud mouth barkeep was right."

"Looks like taking Miller is getting easier."

D. H. Miller stretched himself out on the bunk and covered his eyes with his hands. He was running the day's sounds through his head and putting together in his mind how he thought things would go over the next twenty-four hours. He had heard the church bells this morning, so he knew this was Sunday. He was certain they would move him tomorrow. He figured the Marshal planned to take him by train. Why else wait through the weekend?

Miller had also been paying very close attention to the muffled conversations from outside the jail. There is a morbid curiosity folks have for dangerous people, places, and things. On more than one occasion local gossips had gathered outside the jail's doors to discuss the occupant. Miller learned from the questions and comments that the Marshall had yet to acquire any help in transporting him to Santa Fe. He sifted and sorted all these tidbits of information. You never knew what might be helpful, if the opportunity arose.

TWENTY SIX

At twenty-five minutes past nine on Monday morning, Matt and the Sheriff left El Paso's main bank building. They had spent the last few minutes with the bank's president and vice president inquiring about the money transfers between Marshal John Law and his spies. There wasn't much to learn.

They received a telegram from the Marshal to release certain funds to certain people at various times. The funds came from an account that was set up and maintained through bank drafts. The vice president did confirm; however, that for the past few months the funds were given to a man who wore crooked boots.

After leaving the bank, their next stop was Klein's Dry Goods. They learned from the proprietor that the man who paid with the gold bits had last been on Tuesday afternoon. He purchased what was described as, "trail supplies." It was during this last transaction that Mr. Klein had obtained the gold bit he paid to Matt for setting his arm. Mr. Klein was also able to give them a very detailed description of this customer.

"So, Matt," the Sheriff spoke, "we have a group of men hired to watch another fellow. We don't know anything about the early ones, but we know the last one is dead."

"Yes sir that seems right."

"We also have our mystery man who buys supplies with what appears to be pieces of a gold bar. And you think that gold bar was stolen up in Colorado some five years ago."

"Yeah Sheriff, I do."

"Alright, where do figure our mystery man is now?"

"Hear me out, Albert. This is just my thinking on the situation."

"Go ahead, I promise to be quiet."

"I think the man in question has crossed the border and is headed back north. Remember what James said about the last message to this Marshal?"

"Yeah. He said it was signed as Spotter, but it was a different guy."

"Correct. I think our mystery man sent the message. I think he learned about the Marshal and his spies from the man in the water trough. I think he sent the last telegram."

Sheriff Keating remained silent for a bit, as he digested Matt's theory.

"Matt, I got a problem with that."

"Alright, let's hear it."

"Let's suppose this Marshall wanted this guy, but he

slipped across the border before he could grab him. So, he hires folks to keep an eye on the suspect and inform him if he ever enters his jurisdiction again."

"That's what I think, Sheriff."

"Well then, why would the suspect inform the Marshall that he was back in the country?"

"I think there is some bad blood between those two. I think maybe there are some old wounds. Look, the Marshal in Arizona would not know the telegram came from his suspect. For all he knows, it was from his own man. If he sent it Tuesday afternoon, the Marshal may not have gotten it until Wednesday morning. By that time, the suspect is well on his way. I think he'll be waiting for the Marshal."

"Where will he be waiting for him, Matt?"

"I believe he's gone to where it all started."

"Now, you're doing it again. Where do you think it all started?" Sheriff Keating was getting low on patience.

"If you go due north from here, you will pass just a little east of Silverton, Colorado. Silverton is a short ride southeast of the Ophir mine. The bullion from that robbery has never shown up anywhere. I realize it could have been melted down and spent without any trace, but I believe it is still there nearby."

"I still don't get it. If this mystery man is responsible for the hold up, and if he is going back for his stash, why bring the law down on himself?"

"I don't believe it's just about the gold. I'm convinced it's about settling a score. From a psychological standpoint, these two men are lot alike. They are on different moral planes, but they're both dedicated to a cause, once they start it. Our mystery man knows the Marshal well enough that he's convinced he'll come alone. It's matter of pride. I truly believe he'll be waiting for him in or near Silverton. We need to try to warn him, if we can."

"Well, let's get to James and get a message to Silverton."

TWENTY SEVEN

This Monday morning was one of those that made a person glad to be alive. The sky was clear, without a trace of a cloud. Summer was near, but there was still just enough of spring chill in the air to tingle the senses. John was up and out early. He was more than ready to get this day behind him. If all went according to plan, he figured to be free of Silverton and D. H. Miller by sunrise tomorrow.

Morty was just getting settled for breakfast, as John descended the stairs. He held his travel bag in his left hand and his coat across his right. Bunckus and Gilbert followed close behind. Placing his bag and coat on the floor at the front desk, he turned to the boys.

"You boys ask Miss Sally to fix you something to eat that you can carry with you. I'll be right back. Don't leave here. I will be back."

The boys waited patiently for Miss Sally to exit the kitchen.

Morty nodded acknowledgment, as John approached.

"Morning, Marshal Law."

"Morning, Sheriff. You say the train normally gets here around nine?"

"Pretty close to that."

"Good. I'm going to see the blacksmith. He's supposed to have a pair of shackles ready.

Morty hadn't thought of shackling the prisoner, but he shook his head in agreement.

"I'll meet you there."

Morty couldn't help but notice the "Stick Brothers" talking to Miss Sally.

"Marshal, are you serious about taking them two along?"

"Have you changed your mind about going?"

"No sir."

"Well, neither has anybody else in this town. I'll see you at the jail."

John found it hard to hide his contempt for Morty. He could understand the sheriff not escorting the prisoner, but to show disdain for the only two people in town with the backbone to take his place did not sit well. Morty tried to hide it, but a wave of guilt and shame began to spread over him.

Hal already had the front doors of his shop wide open this morning. A thin veil of smoke filtered out and into the street. In the darkness of the shop, a yellow-orange glow was emanating from the forge. The place was definitely open for business.

"Mawnin, Marshall," came a voice from within. "Is today da day?"

"Today is the day," John responded. "We should have the man down here in about forty five minutes or so."

"Ain't no need in brangin him yere; I got evathang done. All I need do is brang ma chacole bucket an nese small bellas to heat ta rivits. I chain at joker ina jail."

John had considered this method.He most assuredly agreed to it.

"I like that even better. You need help getting things down there?"

"Naw suh. I put it all on a push caat and be right on down."

"Alright, we'll meet you there in half an hour."

The Marshall tipped his hat and left Hal to get things in order.

Bunckus and Gilbert were waiting outside the front door of Miss Sally's when John returned. They had John's things and a fair-sized bag of edibles.

"Miss Sally made you up some food too, Marshal," said Gilbert.

"That's mighty kind of her. Is Morty still inside?"

"No, he just left. He said he would meet us outside the jail. I don't thank he feels too good. He didn't eat nothing, just got up and said he would be at tha jail."

The trio proceeded to the jail.

Miller was lying on the bunk when he heard the key rattle the lock of the front door. Though he looked to be sleeping, he was alert. His eyes were opened just enough to survey who entered. Morty and John brought no interest to him, but the new ones did. D.H. carefully studied the "Stick Brothers." He was certain he had seen them before.

"Rise and shine, Miller," exclaimed Morty. "Your vacation is over." He meant to be received as brave and in charge, but the prisoner was not impressed.

Miller's attention was quickly drawn to a fifth man who entered the room. Hal pushed the door open with his rear end and entered the room backwards. He carried his charcoal bucket in his left hand and held a small bellows in the other. Two iron bracelets, connected together by a short span of chain were draped across his right arm.

He made it through the doorway and turned around, looking for a place to set the bucket of hot coals. Morty moved a chair out of the way and motioned toward the wall on the left side of the entrance. The fireplace took up most of this wall and the hearth was a perfect spot. Hal set the bucket down and turned toward the others. It was then he noticed Bunckus and Gilbert. His eyes lit up with delight.

"Well, It's about time! Which one of yaw is fust? Get ya foot on dis chair." Hal pulled a chair from the table for his workbench.

"It's the man in the cell. We're not chaining these two," responded John.

"Ya sho need to. Oughta chain em up an thow em na river."

"Mr. Hal, wees here ta hep tha Marshal; wees depties," answered Gilbert.

"Depties? Yous ijits is what yous is."

Hal carefully examined the expressions on Morty and John. He was looking for a hint of a joke, but there was none.

"Here's your man," said John, pointing to Miller's cell.

Miller was on his feet staring at Hal. He did not care for black people. The thought of being chained up by one was more than he could bear.

He also hadn't taken into account the use of leg irons. Panic swept over him from his first sight of them. Breaking free would be very difficult. Panic attacks had been hitting him since first being locked up. Convincing himself that he was in charge had helped in ebbing their severity. Now, the fear of being further confined was getting beyond his control.

"That darkie isn't putting his hands on me," he blurted out.

He hated it as he said it. It was a sign of fear. He quietly chastised himself for the infraction.

Hal broke the awkwardness.

"Ain't no need worryin over dat; I always ware ma gloves if I'm ona be handlin a snake. Heh yeh!"

Rage immediately welled up inside Miller. "How dare he insult me?" he thought to himself.

He calmed his anger by formulating his plans for his revenge. He thought of how he would enjoy killing the Marshal. He visualized Bunckus and Gilbert at his mercy, begging for their lives. Morty, he determined, wasn't worth the effort. He would ignore him. This black one though, oh, he planned to spend special time on him.

"I might just use a whole week doing him in," he mused.

The prisoner extended his leg through the bars and stood silent and still for Hal to fasten the shackles. Hal produced a set of tongs from his right coat pocket. From his left he brought out his hammer and two steel rivets.

"Mawty, you take da bellows and blow the coals while I hold these and get em red hot."

"We a hep ya Mr. Hal," volunteered Gilbert.

"If ere one ah yaw two move a anch tawds at fire, Im ona kill da bof a ya," was the response.

Mort picked up the bellows and followed Hal's instructions. The procedure did not take long, and the prisoner was shackled at the ankle and handcuffed at the wrist. John paid Hal and he gathered his things and started to leave. When he reached door, he paused and gave one last look at Bunckus and Gilbert.

"Depties? Heh yeh!"

"We might as well relax until the train gets here," suggested Morty.

"I need to use the slop jar," demanded Miller.

Morty brought the portable toilet bucket out of the closet at the end of the fireplace. Even though it was emptied and rinsed after each use, Morty liked to keep it out of sight. He ordered the prisoner to the back of the cell before opening the access door. John gave full attention to Miller's movements.

"How about some privacy?" asked Miller.

159

"Alright," agreed John. "Boys lets go and wait for the train."

"I need to go too and see if Willie Bee has opened the saloon yet," said Morty.

When all was quiet, D. H. started his preparations. He dropped his pants and thoroughly relieved himself into the slop jar. Before fastening up though, he took the handcuff key he had been hiding from inside his belt and rolled it in a piece of cotton linen torn from his bed sheet.It was uncomfortable, but he gently inserted the wrapped key in his rectum. He left just enough string exposed to extract the key when the time came. Gingerly he rose, pulled up his pants, cinched his belt and waited for the Marshal.

TWENTY EIGHT

The narrow gauge train on its narrow gauge rails slowly puffed its way through the narrow Animas River canyon. If there were any way possible, Odell would push the darn thing to make it reach Silverton faster.

His name was Odell Johnson and keeping a schedule was important to him; maybe even an obsession. Odell took his role as conductor on the Durango to Silverton Line very seriously. But, this morning he was not happy. A rock slide just south of Molas Pass caused them to be behind schedule. It wasn't a major slide and was cleared with very little trouble.

The train though, having come to a complete stop at the foot of the grade, was forced to start up the pass at less than full speed. Nearly all the sand was used up on this one grade, but the little engine managed and Silverton was now in sight. Odell Johnson however, was half an hour behind schedule.

John and the Stick Brothers were waiting at the station when the train arrived. As soon as the hulking beast came to a full stop, Odell began ushering passengers off. He was determined to make up some of his lost time in the turnaround. The brakemen set to work switching cars and making ready for the return trip.

"Now boys, as soon as everyone is off, they'll swap some

cars and turn the engine around. Stay here and pay attention. The conductor will tell you when it's time to get on. You understand?"

"Yes sir."

"Alright, I'm going to get Morty and our prisoner."

"You want us ta hep ya git em, Marshal John?" inquired Gilbert.

"No, you two get on board. Get seated and we'll be along. Here are your tickets."

John left the two on the boarding platform. Surely, these two would be able to manage the simple task of getting on a train. A short time later, all was ready. The boarding call was given and the pair filed on board.

Bunckus and Gilbert had never ridden a train before. The two shared a sense of nervous excitement as they climbed aboard. They sat in the first two empty seats they came to. These seats happened to be the first two in the car.

When Odell entered the compartment he was not his usual tidy self. His uniform was wet with perspiration. Droplets of water covered his face and tiny rivulets streamed down his round, wire-framed, glasses. Trying to save time, he had worked to load and unload the passenger baggage during the switch. In doing so, he had removed his uniform coat and conductor's cap. He hadn't yet put them back on.

Odell was determined to salvage what he could of his schedule. The conductor was stocky, but would not necessarily be considered fat. At five feet six inches tall, his height and weight were well matched. He stood for a moment at the end of the car, catching his breath and watching the passengers get on board. Irritated that they weren't moving faster, he returned to the caboose to dry his face put on his cap and coat.

He cleaned his glasses, retied his bowtie, and was putting the finishing touch to his appearance when a messenger from the ticket office entered and told him to hold the train. Odell didn't take this well.

"Hold the train? He squealed. "We are already behind. No sir-ree. As soon as the water and coal are loaded we're pulling out."

Morty, who had accompanied the messenger, knew Odell. He addressed the irritable old man.

"Odell, keep your steam down. There is a U.S. Marshal and his prisoner riding with you today. I'm going to get him now. Go ahead and get the tickets from everyone else. It will only take long enough to walk to the jail and back."

In truth, Morty was only hoping it would be that quick.

He and John had tried to remove Miller from his cell just moments earlier, only to discover the lock was jammed. Something was stuck in the keyhole. John told him to hurry and hold the train while he went to get Hal. All three returned to the jail at about the same time. Hal was carrying his charcoal bucket and bellows again. After hearing John's description of the problem, he thought he could figure it out.

"There is some kind of metal jammed in the lock," explained John.

"Let me take a peek at it," said Hal, as he knelt down for a closer look.

"Alright you, back against the wall. You know the routine," Morty barked the command to Miller.

"Ats awright Mawty, at big head bowsta put his hains on me, I got sumpim fer him."

Hal took no notice of Miller, as he examined the lock.

"I thank I see what is."

"Can you open the door?" asked John.

"Oh I blieve I can. Mawty, work tha bellows fer me."

Morty picked up the bellows while Hal produced a small, round, steel wire from his coat pocket. He placed it on the coals and worked it back and forth while rolling it. Hal could tell by sight the exact moment the steel reached maximum temperature before starting to melt. When the rod reached a bright, orange-red glow, he took it off the coals and stuck it into the lock. There came a slight sizzling sound from within the lockset and Hal began to blow into it.

"Mawty, brang em bellows and blow into the whole to hep cool it off."

"What is in there"? Marty asked.

"I thank it a piece of a old key. Keys is made ah brass, so if it is a key, it outa melt itself onto tha wire."

After being satisfied things had cooled enough, Hal slowly pulled the wire out.

"Heh yeh! Dare it is," he exclaimed, as he held the wire up for examination.

Sure enough, the wire was welded to the end of the key that D.H. had broken off in the lock his first day in the cell. Miller knew they would eventually open the cell. He did not plan on it being so quick. He was not totally let down. He had, after all, gathered information from watching the proceedings.

He had noticed, for instance, the Sheriff's anxiety. Morty was unable to be still. He looked as though his thoughts were elsewhere. The Marshal looked as though he were finally starting to wear down. Miller saw for the first time a touch of panic in the old lawman.

John's mind was, indeed, a flood of thought. If the train left without them, he hadn't worked out an alternate plan. Internally, he was chastising himself for not searching the prisoner when they first locked him up. He would be sure to remedy that before Miller was taken out.

"Mawty, you can git em out now...yaw need anythang else?"

"No, Hal, much obliged," answered Morty.

Hal collected his things and left the jail for the second time that day.

Odell stood on the platform at the back of the caboose looking towards the jail. His attention was drawn to the cattle car hooked directly behind him. It was not unusual to haul livestock. The mines were in constant need of pack and draft animals. There were a few guide services that used mules to ferry paying guests on a short trip into the mountains. What captivated his thoughts were the exceptional riding horses in the car. Tethered to the rail at the far end were two of the finest animals he had ever seen. They were very easy to notice among the mules and burros in the car. The horses were eye catching on their own, but these two were even more out of place, because they were both saddled and bridled.

Odell's first thought was a robbery. He had ridden the rails for a long time and the threat of bandits was always on his mind. Was someone planning to stop the train, grab the valuables, and make a run for it?

"We're only carrying passengers," he said to himself.

Gold and silver bullion was shipped once a month in a special armored rail car. The shipment for June was completed two weeks ago. It would be another two before July's load was picked up.

The mystery would have to wait; there were tickets to punch. Odell walked through the caboose and into the next passenger car. The first seats he came to were occupied by Bunckus and Gilbert.

"Tickets please, give me your tickets," he announced.

The conductor did not understand the blank stares from the boys.

"Give me your tickets, boys."

"Why, ain't you got yer own?" Gilbert responded.

"I'm not in the mood for foolishness. Give me your tickets, so I can punch you."

The boys exchanged a quick glance with each other.

"Boys, if I don't punch you, you can't ride the train." Odell's voice was rising with his temper.

"You punch me and I'm ona knock a knot on yer head," replied Gilbert.

"Yeah," added Bunckus. "an an an I ah ah kick oo butt."

Odell truly thought the boys were teasing him, and he was not in any state of mind for it. Without thinking it through, he committed one of those spontaneous acts that folks often do and immediately regret. Noticing the ticket protruding from Gilbert's shirt pocket, he snatched it out and was about to punch it, but never got the chance. Within the blink of an eye, Odell's bad day took a substantial turn for the worse.

When Morty and John entered the car with Miller between them, chaos met them. The boys were up and sticks were flying. Women were screaming and babies were crying. John shoved the prisoner into the empty seat to his right and sat on him as he ascertained what had happened. Morty grabbed a man in each hand and unleashed a torrent of profanities on them. This gave Odell a chance to get to his feet. He quickly lit in to the boys.

"Out! Out! Out! Get out of my car! Get off my train! Out! Out! Out!"

Morty's mind raced for a solution. Taking the prisoner

back to the jail was not one of them.

"Odell, these two are escorting the Marshal and his prisoner. I'll take care of them as soon as they get back."

"They are back already, because they are not going. Out! Out! Out!"

Odell had lost control. His face was as red as Hal's charcoal fire. His neck was swollen with rage. It looked as though his bowtie would pop any minute. He was screaming in an uncontrollable pitch.

"We'll ride in the cattle car," John suggested.

"No way, I'm not putting those animals in with the livestock," Odell retorted.

"Listen to me pal. I'm a United States Marshal conveying a Federal prisoner. I can commandeer this whole train if need be." John was gambling on that last threat.

"Oh yeah, well you and your prisoner can go to h…"

"Alright, Odell, you are right," interrupted Morty, "You have been assaulted and I need to take proper action. I'm taking these two to jail. Follow me down and we will fill out your complaint."

"I'm not going anywhere. We're already behind schedule. This train is pulling out."

169

That's all Morty was waiting to hear.

"This train is where the crime took place. It is not moving until we can complete the investigation. I have to interview any witnesses that want to come forward and write down what they say. It shouldn't take but a couple of hours."

Silence finally returned to the compartment. Odell struggled to suppress the urge to grab one of the sticks and use it on Morty.

"Never mind, then. You got one minute…that's sixty seconds, to get in the car. As soon as I verify the other tickets, this train is leaving. You got one minute"

John got up from the prisoner and proceeded to hurry him out the door. He turned to motion for the others to follow. That's when he noticed the two strangers. They were sitting down front pretending to be unconcerned. John's inner voice was calling loud and clear. He had seen their horses and knew they had no need of the train. There was no doubt in his mind. They were shadowing him.

Odell picked up his cap and straightened his hair as best he could before placing it back on. Still seething with rage, he turned and continued punching tickets. It was a race with him now, he determined to finish before John, his prisoner, and the Stick Brothers could board the livestock car.

Morty exited the train first. He was followed by Miller, who was firmly ushered along by John. Bunckus and Gilbert stepped off last. The Sheriff and the boys were confused when John did not immediately reboard the last car.

"Change of plans. Follow me," he commanded, as he walked past them.

TWENTY NINE

John hurried his entourage along as fast as a chained man could be hurried. They walked past the last rail car and headed to Hal's shop. He was hoping to get inside and out of sight without being seen by anyone on board the train.

As soon as the group reached Hal's they heard the whistle of the train, but this was not the outbound one. Down the tracks an incoming engine was approaching. Unknown to John beforehand, during the tourist season the railroad ran two, and sometimes three, locomotives a day between Durango and Silverton.

The delays encountered by the first one had allowed the second one to catch up. Odell and his group would have to sit still while the brakemen switched the second train to the side tracks. John smiled quietly to himself. The thought of the conductor's schedule being further soured brought a touch of joy.

Hal was busy forging horseshoes when the Marshall and crew arrived.

"I thought yaw wuz gone"?

"Change of plans," John said.

There was a straight-backed wooden chair in front of the center support post of the blacksmith shop. It's placement in this particular spot was not accidental. When work was slow, Hal occupied the chair and leaned it against the post for a short nap. John pushed the chair against the post and shoved D.H. into it. Miller didn't like the rough treatment, but took it quietly. He mentally added each infraction for recompense as soon as he got free.

"Got any rope"? Asked John.

"Gots planty," answered Hal, as he tossed John a bundle hanging just above the anvil where he was.

John tied the prisoner, chair and all, to the post. He wrapped ample loops of rope around his chest, waist, knees, and ankles. When he was confident the man was secure, he turned and addressed the others.

"Gilbert and Morty, you stay here and keep a close eye on him. Bunckus, you come with me. Hal, take the shackles off of him."

"Take 'em off? Why da rivits ain't cooled good from when I put 'em on im is mawning."

"I don't have time, just get them off."

John and Bunckus were leaving the shop as one of the waitresses from the Outcrop entered.

"Excuse me, have you seen Morty"?

"I'm here, Darlene," answered Morty.

"Why, I been looking all over for you. Miss Sally said you were at the jail. I looked there, but you weren't in. Somebody said they saw you at the train depot, so I went down there, but the man at the ticket office said you went in here. By the way, what did you do to the conductor? You can hear him cussing you from the platform."

"Darlene, never mind all that what do you want"?

"Oh, it's Willie Bee. He fell out the back door when he went to empty the mop water. I thank he broke his leg or something."

Morty glanced from John, to Hal, to the prisoner, and back to John. He was at a loss as to which way to go or what to do. Finally, Hal spoke up.

"Yaw go on. I got tis joker. He ain't goin no whare."

Morty hurried to the Outcrop Saloon. He was glad to be away from Miller. John and Bunckus left and proceeded down the street to the livery stable.

After a few minutes they returned with Bunckus riding his horse and leading Gilbert's. The plan was to put Miller on one and let the boys double up. John was riding the rented horse. This was the third time he had rented the animal, but the first time he had been in the saddle. It was a very fine mount indeed, he thought to himself. Halfway between the jail and the saloon, as John was watching the train finally leave the station, they met Morty hurrying toward them. The trio stopped as they met.

"Are you taking him on horseback?" asked the Sheriff.

"I think my best choice now is heading west to Rico, then on down to Dolores. We can board the train there."

"That's a long way around. What was wrong with the train"?

"It will take too long to explain. We have to get moving. What about Willie Bee"?

"Ah, just sprained his ankle I think. I'm going to have Doc look at him. You need help with Miller"?

"No, I think we can manage."

Morty was quiet for a moment. Guilt and fear were gnawing at him. He began to wish he had some of the grit he saw in this Marshal.

"Godspeed, Marshal. Telegraph me when you get to Dolores."

John nodded in agreement. He was still carrying his travel bag. He opened it now; pulling a black, double holster with hand-stitched leather from it. He balanced the bag across the saddle while he fastened the holster around his waist. It had been a while, but it still felt like it belonged there. Next, he retrieved his two double-action, .45 caliber Colt Model 1878's.

John loved these weapons and was well acquainted with them. He had modified the trigger springs to make them very easy to fire. The slightest finger pressure brought them alive.

He checked the cylinder and placed the right one where it belonged. He did the same with the left, but as he pulled the thin, rawhide, tie-down strap, it broke. This small piece of leather string was meant to loop around the hammer of the pistol to secure it in the scabbard. He pulled the gun out to see if he could make a quick repair. Untying it required both hands, so John handed the loaded weapon to Bunckus.

From Morty's perspective everything went into slow motion. No matter how fast he tried to move, he was unable to stop Bunckus from touching the pistol. Morty's worst fear was immediately realized. Bunckus grabbed the gun, trigger first, and the mindless piece of equipment functioned exactly as it was designed to.

There was an almost deafening boom as the hammer hit the center of the cartridge and exploded. The bullet shot from the end of the four and a half inch barrel in an instant. The projectile grazed John trousers just above his knee and traveled, unheeded, into the heart of the rented horse. The animal dropped straight down where it had been standing.

Morty made his way around and grabbed the gun before any further rounds were let loose. He immediately started in on Bunckus with a flurry of profanities. John was still sitting in the saddle of the now dead horse.

The nearby citizens who had taken cover, slowly came out of hiding. John rose up from the saddle and, without any sound or display of emotion, walked down the boardwalk toward the Outcrop Saloon. He entered the swinging doors walked directly by the waitresses and tables, and straight to the bar. Willie Bee was sitting on a low stool against the back wall soaking his foot in a basin of hot water.

John paid no attention to him or anyone else. He went to the bar and picked up the nearest bottle of whiskey. Removing the cork, he took three deep swallows without blinking. He set the bottle back in place, but then lifted it again for another shot. This time he replaced the cork, set the bottle down and left in the same silent manner as he had entered. Willie Bee watched the entire event without any of his usual commentary.

When John returned to the scene of the carnage a crowd had gathered. In the middle of the group was Ben. He was livid over the death of the horse. Waving his hands and stopping one foot, he was demanding retribution for his loss. Morty's attempts to calm him were to no avail. Ben noticed

John approaching and let loose on him with equal fervor.

"What in God's name is going on here, Marshal? You rent the horse, you bring it back. You rent it again and you bring it back. You rent it again, but now you can't bring it back because you done killed it. You are going to pay me for this horse!"

"I'll make it right," answered John.

"You're damn right you'll make it right! That was the best horse I rented out." It was, in fact, the only horse he had.

"I don't have time your yelling right now," said John. "Name your price and shut up."

"That there horse was worth five hundred dollars!"

John returned the quote with a cold, penetrating stare that struck Ben to the center of his soul. He was looking into the face of man who, at his core, was as solid as stone. It shook him. Whether real or imagined, Ben believed his very life was hanging on the next thing he said. Slowly and calmly he answered.

"I think fifty will settle it."

John turned to Morty. "Sheriff, you witness that I owe this man fifty dollars."

Morty nodded in agreement and John turned his attention to Bunckus, who was still crying from Morty's berating.

"Get back to the stable, harness the horses to the wagon and meet me at the blacksmith shop."

"You'll need a double tree hook up for that. Come on, I'll fix you up," volunteered Ben. He was desperate for a reason to leave this scene.

John took his gun from Morty and put it in his left coat pocket. "I still plan to take the west route to Rico."

As he walked back to Hal's, John was going over in his mind the itinerary of the train. He remembered there being three flag stops on the route. The first was Elk Park, about thirty minutes from town. The next was Needleton, about one hour out. John was certain that, if the strangers on the train planned to take the prisoner, it would be at one of these stops.

"Lord, let them wait until the last one," He prayed.

The prayer caused him to stop in the street. It had been a long time since he had entertained any idea of divine intervention. He was not sure why he sought it now.

THIRTY

John became alarmed when he saw Hal's shop was closed. He drew his gun and approached from the side. After creeping the last few steps to the corner of the building and once in position at the side, he kicked the main entrance door.

"Is at you, Marshal John?" Gilbert whispered through the planks.

"Yes. Who's in there with you?"

"Just Hal and tha prisner. Are you alright?"

"I'm fine. Open the door."

With the sound of the main bolt being drawn back and the creak of the hinges, the door swung out. John stepped around and inside. Shock is the only way to describe his expression. Gilbert met him with a short, double-barreled, shotgun. This particular one was the Triple Wedge hammerless Greener. On these models, both barrels were automatically cocked as soon as the breech was closed. Looking to the rear of the shop he saw Hal holding an identical weapon at Miller's head.

"We heard a shot and wudn't show what wuz goin on," explained Hal.

"Minor accident, everything's fine."

"I figgered maybe 'em two fancy jokers on 'em fancy hawses was trying to git tis fella. I decided if they came yere, all they wuz gonna git is pieces uf 'em. Hey yeh!"

John was surprised that anyone else had taken notice of the two strangers.

"Oh, I seen 'em scannels when ney fust rode in. They thawt they wuz slick, an foolin somebody, but I can spot a fox in a hen house. You seed 'em too, didn't ya?"

"I noticed them."

"Well, I ain't show what tay up to, but it ain't no good."

"I don't have time to find out now. I need you to put the leg irons back on the prisoner, and I need you to hurry."

It was Hal's turn to display an expression of shock.

"I jus got em off. Jus set ma hamma down when we hear da gun shoot."

"There isn't time to explain, just get him shackled."

Hal set the shotgun down on the bench and started working the bellows to heat up another set of rivets.

"Chain na man, an nen unchain na man, an nen chain em up again. How in da wuld did you white folks eva git in chaage a dis country"?

Hal was hammering the last rivet flat as Bunckus arrived

with the wagon. He stepped back as John and Gilbert untied Miller and stood him on his feet. D.H. made a quick glance at the shotgun on the work bench. Hal noticed.

"You want it? Git it. But you won't never live ta pick it up."

Miller gave another quick glance at the hammer in Hal's right hand and changed his mind. It was a fleeting thought of desperation anyway. He reminded himself that he could not show any such weakness to these lesser individuals.

Hal took the other shotgun from Gilbert, placing it and the hammer beside the other one on the bench. He then started helping John and Gilbert load the prisoner. Miller twisted his shoulders away from Hal's grasp.

"Keep your black paws off me."

"Aright, I won't touch you."

Hal stepped in front of Miller, reached down, grasped the chains he was shackled with and yanked them up with all his might. The outlaw's feet followed the force up and out, landing him flat on his back in the dust. Without hesitation, Hal proceeded to drag him through the dust to the waiting wagon. Reaching it, he dropped the chains and cast his gloves aside. Before Miller could recover himself, Hal, with bare hands, grabbed him by the shoulders and lifted him to his feet as if he were a child.

"Awe, look, I done got you dirty." He then intentionally put his hands on Miller from his head to his waist. Miller attempted to lunge for Hal, but John and Gilbert already had him in hand.

"I'm going to kill you. As soon as I'm free of these chains, I'm going to come for you."

"All you goin do is git in at wagon. You goin in yaself, or I gotta hep ya?"

John and Gilbert had a firm grip on the prisoner by then. With Bunckus' help, they loaded him in the wagon. Bunckus took charge of tying him. He liked tying knots.

John filled Hal in on the planned route and asked him to keep an eye out. If he thought they were being followed, he was to inform Morty. He wasn't sure what good that would do.

When all looked ready, the Marshal got in the back of the wagon with Bunckus and Miller. He noticed Ben had supplied grain and a bit of hay for the horses. With Gilbert at the reins they proceeded on their way.

THIRTY ONE

The Marshal, his prisoner, and the deputies reached the south end of town as the second train was leaving the station. John made a mental note that it was about half an hour behind the first. The group turned west and headed the wagon back up the South Mineral Trail.

Odell was very pleased when his train reached Elk Park. There wasn't anyone standing beside the tracks to flag the train down. The engineer kept full steam and rumbled on south. The second stop at Needleton was not so fortunate.

Standing beside the rail with a burrow in tow, there stood a grizzled old miner waving his hands across his knees. To Odell's great consternation, the engineer began easing the throttle and applying the brakes. The train halted and the two strangers decided to make their move. They rose and exited the rear of the passenger car, on each side of the rails. With guns drawn they carefully approached the cattle car. In unison they climbed the ladders and shouted into the car.

"Nobody move!"

None of the animals responded. The two surveyed the car from front to back, looking for the Marshal and his crew.

"They're not here," commented the taller one.

"That lawman spotted us in town. They never got

184

onboard," responded the shorter one. "Drop the ramp...let's unload the horses and head after them."

Meanwhile, Odell was hurrying to get the gang plank down for the miner and his burrow. He thought the strangers had volunteered to give him a hand. But the two simply brushed past him as soon as the board dropped, leading their horses back northward. Odell and the miner shared profanities with them, but they kept walking. After a slight struggle, the burrow was loaded and Odell was off again. The strangers halted after the train left.

"There was a second train at the station. They could be on it," surmised the taller. "Let's wait here and check it before we make the ride back."

Thirty minutes later they flagged it down. With guns drawn, they searched both passenger cars. Satisfied John had changed routes, they headed back to Silverton.

"Should we climb up to the road and cut them off?"

"No, if he thinks we're after him, he won't go south."

"Which way, then?"

"The road north of Silverton is kind of rough, and once you get out of the mountains, you're still a long ways from help. The trail east is more difficult and doesn't give much chance of help either. I'd say he was heading west. There's another rail head in Dolores. If I was him, that's where I would be going."

"Well, its noon now. We best make tracks."

The pair headed back to Silverton as fast as conditions would allow. The loose ballast along the tracks and fording the Animas River more than once made the journey time-consuming. It was nearly five o'clock in the afternoon when they made it back to town. The horses were exhausted from the extra pushing required of them. The strangers slowly rode to the livery stable, trying not to be noticed. Ben was about to close up shop when they approached.

"Can we impose upon you to take care of our animals before you lock up?" Asked the taller again.

Ben looked them over for a moment. His first inclination was to say no, but those two beautiful horses looking so completely worn out changed his mind.

"If you will remove the riggins, I'll feed and water them. After I get done with my supper I'll come back and brush them down for you too."

"Much obliged."

After the horses were taken care of the strangers walked down to the Outcrop Saloon. They did not take the main street. They went down the alley behind the buildings. Their first stop was the jail. Stealthily, they crept up to the bars. There were no lights or sounds from within. They found a barrel nearby and rolled it up to the window to stand on for a better look between the bars. The place was empty.

"Isn't anybody here, Ab," said the shorter of the two.

"I didn't think there would be, but we had to make sure. That has-been lawman has left town with him."

"You still think he will try for Dolores?"

"Yep, and they got about a six hour start on us. While the horses recover, let's ease on down to the saloon and see if that loud mouth barkeep can tell us anything."

At the first alley the two crossed over to the main street and proceeded down the boardwalk to the Outcrop. Morty was tending bar. He didn't see them on the train and thus, did not connect them to the Marshal or his prisoner. The strangers innocently nodded to him as they entered. Morty returned the gesture and pointed to two empty stools to his right. They took their seats, removed their hats and ordered drinks like everyone else.

"Where is the guy who usually pours the poison?"

"Oh, he took a fall out the back door this morning; busted up his ankle a bit. I got him resting up over in his room. Doc says he should be fine in a day or so."

"He's got a room here in the bar?"

"No," replied Morty, "he'd drink me poor. No, he's got a small room down the street."

Within a few minutes of what Morty thought was innocent conversation; the strangers learned the exact location of Willie Bee. They told Morty they were leaving town early in the morning and asked for a bottle whiskey for the trail. Without any reservations, Morty complied. The strangers left the saloon and headed straight to Willie Bee's place with the bottle in hand.

It didn't take long to get Willie loosened up enough to tell all he knew. They learned of the Stick Brothers, the dead horse, the wagon, and even the route. Twenty minutes later, the horses were fed, watered, and brushed down. The animals could have used several hours of rest, but time wouldn't allow it. They saddled up and left in pursuit of Marshal John.

Hal noticed the pair when they first arrived back, and had been keeping up with them the whole time. As soon as they passed his shop, he headed to get Morty. He explained to the Sheriff all he and the Marshal suspected of the two. Morty was more than a little alarmed. He was also very disgusted with himself for not paying more attention to the entire situation.

Hal also enlightened Morty about the strangers having visited Willie Bee. He did not need to say more. Morty put it all together. He had unwittingly betrayed the Marshal and maybe even endangered his life. Another wave of fear and regret swept over him with the thought that he had maybe even turned a killer loose again.

"Now Mawty, I'm ona saddle ma mule and git afta 'em. Is you comin"?

"What good is following them going to do?"

"I plan on ketchin' 'em an stoppin' 'em."

Morty desperately searched for a reason not to go. "I don't have anybody to run this place."

Hal leaned his head back and just silently stared at him. Morty got the message.

"Alright, the girls can close up. I'll saddle up and meet you at your shop. I'll also have to stop by the jail and get you a badge."

"Ah badge? What fer"?

"Well, I have to deputize you."

"Naw you ain't. If you deptize me, I'll have to folla da law. Heh Yeh!"

Hal left without further discussion. Morty knew the

subject of deputizing the man was a non-starter. He instructed the waitresses to close as early as possible, and left to get ready.

Hal was sitting on his mule, armed with his two Greener shotguns when Morty finally came riding down the street. Just before he reached the blacksmith shop, Elbert, the telegraph operator, ran up to him.

"Hey Morty, you seen that Marshal that's been hanging around here?"

Morty was not really sure how to answer him, so he told just part of the truth.

"He bought tickets for the train this morning."

"Well, I've been looking all over for him; got a message this morning for him."

"Let me have it. I'll see it's taken care of."

Morty took the small, yellow envelope and tucked it into his pocket. The operator noticed that Mort was fitted out for the trail. He also noticed Hal waiting in the shadow of the shop.

"You two headin' out somewhere?"

"Thought we might go varmint hunting for a spell."

Elbert noticed Morty wearing his pistol and Hal carrying

two shotguns.

"Awful lot of weapons for varmints, isn't it? They must be terrible big."

"Good night, Elbert," answered Morty as he and Hal rode away.

Hal paused at the end of town, just before turning west onto the road. He listened for a moment before speaking.

"Them two got about fawty minutes head start. They cain't move too fast in the dark, but once at full moon gits above dem hills, it gonna be bright as day. We need to ride quiet and make time…want to catch 'em afo they know we afta 'em."

"It's going to be pitch black once we get out of town all the way."

"Just ride slow and steady, we a git em."

Hal handed one of the shotguns to Morty. It was loaded with 12-gauge double-ought buckshot and the breach was open.

"Dat's a hammaless model. All ya gotta do is close it and it's ready to fire."

"I got it, let's go."

THIRTY TWO

The horses weren't making much progress pulling the wagon, supplies, and four men. They had to stop rest them roughly every hour. John was desperate to travel on, but the animals were exhausted. At ten o'clock he told Gilbert to pull up when he found a suitable spot; a short while later, Gilbert eased the team off the road and into a small clearing.

The moon was full and filled the area with ample light to unhitch the horses and feed them. John paid close attention to any sounds from behind them. He had no way of knowing if they were being followed or not. His instincts told him they were. The prisoner was taken from the wagon and tied to a slender Ponderosa pine at the edge of the clearing. Bunckus made several loops of rope around Miller before cinching them tightly and tying the knots behind the tree.

Even with his hands free, it would be nearly impossible for Miller to untie himself. John made certain the murderous outlaw was kept in the moonlight as much as possible. He found himself a well-concealed area near the road. The plan was to have Miller exposed while he sat in the shadows.

"Marshal John, are we gonna stay here all night?" asked Gilbert.

"We'll stay as long as the horses need to. They're about

worn out."

"Yeah, they's tired alright. They ain't used to pulling is much load."

"Well, let them eat and get some water and rest. You boys grab a bite yourselves. I'll keep watch."

Bunckus double checked the ropes on the prisoner and returned to the wagon. Every so often he checked the underbrush for movement. He still had fears of being slowly eaten alive. Gilbert made sure the horses were taken care of and joined him.

John took his position in the brush and Miller sat quiet and still. He was listening to sound also. He knew the Marshal was worried, which gave him the opportunity to set his mind on getting free.

The scene grew quiet except for the natural sounds of a mountain forest at night. John was drifting off to sleep when a shout from the wagon jolted him.

"Dangit Bunckus, watch them toe claws of yours! Why'd ja take ya shoes off anyhow?"

"My, ah ah my ah feet hurt."

"Well, put 'em back on afore ya stab me ta death."

Quiet resumed and it wasn't long before Gilbert was

snoring. This was a sound that Miller took note of. He could neither see nor hear the Marshal.

John intently listened to the road toward Silverton. Years of listening had taught him how to discern what was natural from what was manmade. He fought off fatigue as best he could, but after an hour of listening, he drifted off again.

Miller was still awake and still listening. He was sure Gilbert was asleep. The Marshal was a mystery to him, but he surmised he was asleep also. There had been no sounds of movement for quite some time from John's position. From his rope shackles, he could hear Bunckus mumbling to himself, so he determined he was sleeping. Slowly, he began to make his move. With planned, smooth motion, he loosened his belt.

But Bunckus had not been asleep. A crack between the planks of the wagon's sideboards gave him a very good view of the prisoner, and Bunckus paid very close attention to every move he made. He noticed Miller unfastening his belt and then his pants. Miller then pulled his feet in and raised himself slightly off the ground.

Bunckus had his hand on his stick and was ready to pounce if the outlaw got up. Miller did not try to get up though, he rose up just enough to get his pants lowered to reach his hiding place. Bunckus watched him reach his hands down between his thighs and remove a small cloth packet from a place he could not believe. In disbelief, he continued watching as Miller unfolded the packet and removed a key.

Tossing the cloth over his shoulder, he placed the key into the keyhole for the handcuffs. The key turned and the cuffs opened. Bunckus moved to attack, but stopped when he saw Miller relock the handcuffs. He raised his pants, fastened his belt and stretched out to sleep.

"Gibbert, Gibba Gibba Gibba Gibbert."

"Dang it, Bunckus, what's a matter with you"?

"At ah ah ah at cookie tomper got a key."

Gilbert quietly rose up to check on the prisoner. All was still and the man appeared to be sleeping.

"Bunckus, you're crazy. Ever body is asleep and you need to be."

"Gibbert, he ah he got a key. I cheed it."

"Just where did he git a key then?"

"He ah ah he took it outa he butt."

Gilbert stared at Bunckus as he fought back a tremendous urge to slap him.

"Out of his butt?"

"I cheed it. He ah ah ah took it outa he butt. What we

gone ah what we gone do"?

"Well, I'm going back to sleep, you keep watching and see where he hides his lock."

Gilbert rolled over and left Bunckus watching.

THIRTY THREE

The full moon gave ample light for the strangers in their pursuit of Law and his party. In fact, it gave a bit too much light. They held to the shadows at every opportunity and carefully scanned the road ahead as they pushed on after their prey. They knew John was armed, so they needed to get as close as possible before being seen.

Something else the moonlight did well was illuminate the wagon and horse tracks in the road. There were areas where boot prints were mingled around the hoof prints. This could only mean that the team had stopped and tended to the horses.

"Ab, looks like those poor horses are getting spent."

"Yeah, we might be closer than we think. Let's walk for a spell."

The pair dismounted and slowly crept down the road; listening carefully for any sound ahead.

It was to Hal and Morty's benefit the strangers were preoccupied with the road in front of them. They gave hardly any notice to their being followed. Hal spotted them about a half hour previously. He motioned for Morty to remain as quiet as possible and stay out of sight. Surprise was vital to their success also. This cat and mouse game continued as the man in the moon looked on in silence.

John was awakened by the sound of a twig snapping. He did not move from his covered position. He listened more intently for further sounds while berating himself for drifting off to sleep. The moon was gone and, judging by the predawn gray surrounding him, he knew sunrise was not far off. Another twig snapped and this time he saw the culprit. A large red squirrel had jumped from one tree to another and nearly missed the branch it was aiming for.

John hurriedly and quietly moved from his position and woke the boys. In a whisper he gave instructions to harness the horses as silently as possible, while he untied and brought the prisoner. Miller pretended to be asleep, but he watched the Marshal approach.

"Alright, on your feet, it's time to move."

Miller sat still while John untied him and assisted him to his feet.

"Need to answer a call of nature first."

John, with great irritation, lifted the man to his feet and, with his hand firmly on his neck, led him into the trees a short distance. Miller locked the handcuffs back on himself last night, but they were only to the first click. Unless a person checked closely, they would not have known they were loose.

As soon as the wagon was out of sight, Miller slipped his hands free and took full advantage of his daily exercises. He spun to his left, crushing the unsuspecting Marshal with a right hand as he did so. The blow sent John to the ground. D.H. reached for the lawman's gun as he fell. His hand touched the butt of the pistol, but that's as far as he got. His world went dark.

Gilbert came down on the back of the outlaw's head with an equally crushing blow of his stick. John was dazed, but recovered himself enough to see Gilbert standing over the unconscious man.

"Bunckus said that joker had a key, but I just couldn't hardly blieve it."

"Where did he get a key?" John was still a bit dazed.

Gilbert paused for a moment.

"You will hafta ask Bunckus...I still ain't blievin at part."

Gilbert grabbed the chains of the shackles and proceeded to drag Miller back to the wagon. John followed along to the wagon. He was relieved and aggravated. Gilbert had just saved the lives of these three men. How could he, a Marshal, not have been more aware of the situation? He had searched the prisoner thoroughly before he took him out of the cell.

He would definitely ask Bunckus about that key. A knot was forming in his stomach as he pondered how terrible his misjudgment could have been.

"Maybe I am past it," he thought.

THIRTY FOUR

With daylight fast approaching, Hal made the decision to follow on foot. He and Morty tied their mounts out of site of the road and cautiously began stalking the strangers. After only a short distance they came upon a pile of fresh horse manure.

"Em jokers is close, Mawty."

"Yeah, and when the sun comes up, we're going to be out in the open on this road. You been to Rico before, haven't you?"

"Sho' have, you know that."

"You know then that he road runs downhill here and follows the creek for about half a mile. It then turns right and goes uphill to the last ridge before town."

"Yep, my ole mule has done clambed at hill many times."

"Then you know that if we cut across this ridge, we'll save that half mile down and half mile back. We might even come out in front of them. What do you think?"

"I thank you right, but it's gonna be tough."

"Not as rough as running into them on this open road."

"Let's get going den."

Morty led the way as they started their attack on the ridge.

It was steep and part of it required hands and knees. They kept a fair pace and were soon at the top. After a short rest, they proceeded down the other side.

The descent was almost as difficult. They had to be very careful with each step; tripping over a root or stepping into a hole almost guaranteed broken ankle at the least. It took nearly half an hour to clear the ridge and get back to the road.

There were no signs of anyone having traveled this way lately. They had managed to get ahead of the group. It was now a matter of getting back down the road without being seen and maybe getting to John before the strangers did.

Hal took the right side of the road and Morty took the left. They eased along as quickly as stealth would allow. After about twenty minutes, Morty signaled for Hal to hold up. He heard voices. It was impossible to determine whether friend or foe, so they sat and listened for a moment. They agreed to leave the road and proceed along the edge of the trees. This made progress slower, but it provided cover.

Another ten minutes passed and Morty called to hold up again. The two men sat and listened to the voices, trying to determine the distant to them.

A shot rang out!

THIRTY FIVE

Miller was still semi-conscious when Gilbert got him back to the tree. He searched him, took the handcuff key and placed it in his pants pocket. The outlaw was slowly coming to as Gilbert finished tying the knots and then went to help Bunckus hitch the horses.

John stood in the middle of the clearing. He could see the boys at the horses and also had a good view of Miller. There was another twig snapping, but this was too close to be a squirrel. His hand went to his pistol, but before he touched it, the cold, hard barrel of a forty-four was pressed into his neck.

"Don't move lawman." The strangers had caught up.

"You two over there, get away from the horses. Get over in front of the wagon. If you got guns, throw them over here...real slow."

"We ain't got no guns," said Gilbert.

"Keep your hands where we can see them. Now you, Marshal Has-Been, take your left hand and, ever-so-gently undo your gun belt and hold it out away from you."

John complied and took off his holster. He held it out in his left hand.

"Del, come take his rig, and check that wagon for any

others."

The shorter of the two took John's weapon and dropped it to the ground beside the wagon. Feeling the scene was in their control, the taller of the pair began his speech.

"Marshal, you cost us a lot of wasted time. What do you think you're doing here anyway?"

"I've come to arrest a criminal and take him back to stand trial. How did you two show up in this?"

"My name is Abercrombie…Luis Abercrombie. Folks call me Ab. That fellow there is Delbert Swindoll. We've been bringing desperadoes in for about ten years now. A little bird told us about D. H. coming back into circulation. We're going to take him in. You should have stayed out of it."

Miller was back to his senses and was a bit pleased with the turn of events. Ab noticed he was watching and listening.

"Oh course now, you, Mr. Miller, might have some say in how this turns out. There is a one thousand dollar reward for you. There is also a rumor that you have a substantial fortune hid around here. Me and my partner might be willing to deal with you."

"If you think you can deal with this snake…," started John.

"Shut up Marshal! I'm in charge here."

Miller sat silently.

"What about it, convict? You want to deal or go to jail?"

"I don't deal with fools," replied Miller.

"Fools? We aren't the ones handcuffed, shackled, and tied to a tree."

Miller could see that greed was consuming the two bounty hunters. They could be easily duped once he was free. John Law would have to be subdued first. That man would never give in, otherwise.

"You boys are fools, alright. You took the Marshal's gun outfit...did you look at it?"

Ab and Del looked at the holster on the ground. The realization of their error hit them at the same time. John's holster was a double rig, but only one gun was in it.

Turning back to John, Ab demanded, "alright, where is it?"

John was furious with Miller. He had been waiting for an opportunity to get his gun and regain control of the situation. Now that hope was gone.

"It's in my coat pocket."

"Well, you just take it out of your coat pocket and hand it over; real slow, with your left hand. And it had better come out barrel first too."

John gingerly pulled the gun out and held it between his thumb and two fingers.

"You, little one, go get it," said Ab, pointing to Bunckus.

John prayed that Bunckus was consistent. He held the weapon out and was very careful to point the barrel away from them. Bunckus walked over and took the pistol.

Just like the previous occasion, Bunckus grasped the weapon trigger first. This time John was ready. As soon as the blast went off, he leaped over Bunckus and, with his right hand, took out all his frustration on Ab's left jaw.

The bounty hunter dropped where he had been standing. Gilbert was also ready. Before Del could recover from the sudden noise of the percussion, he retrieved his stick and had his man down beaten to a pulp.

John quickly returned to Bunckus and took the gun. Bunckus had an expression of horror and was staring silently at the man tied to the tree. There was a growing crimson stain coming down the front of Miller's shirt. The bullet Bunckus fired had passed through the lower part of his heart. With every beat, the organ was now pumping his life away.

Miller's world began to swirl and spin away. There came a

rushing sound to his ears, and the mountain clearing gave way to cloudy visions from the past. He heard the voices and saw the faces of many of his victims. In rapid succession they appeared and faded.

He saw the water trough and a little Mexican girl. There appeared the gold haulers from Ophir and the family from Taos. His father came and vanished, as did the Kiowa. His mother's face came into view. She was young as he remembered her as a child. Her image paused and lingered. He reached for her, but she faded away into darkness.

John and the Stick Brothers watched his deathly hands reach out for something that was not there. After a brief moment, they dropped, lifeless, into his lap. His head crashed to his chest and he slumped to his left side as far as the ropes would allow.

With neither fanfare nor final words, D.H. Miller slipped into eternity.

THIRTY SIX

Ab slowly began to recover from John's blow. He rose to his feet and noticed Miller.

"Well, that tears it!" he exclaimed.

John quickly turned and covered him with his pistol.

"Get your sidekick up and both of you stand by the wagon."

"Put the gun down and give it up lawman. Miller isn't worth anything dead."

It was true. In D.H. Miller's long criminal career, he had never been arrested; much less charged or convicted. He was suspected in several grisly murders and thus, all rewards were for his capture to stand trial.

"Worthless or not, he's yours. Take him back to Silverton and fill out the paperwork."

"No deal. He's your prisoner. Me and Del are leaving him with you and your deputies."

"You two will take him or you will not get your guns back. And I'll get you on charges of interfering with an officer of the law. I'm doing the charitable thing here in giving you the chance to walk."

"Officer of the law…"

The conversation was silenced by the metal-on-metal click from the breech of a shotgun being closed.

"I spec you betta do what ta main says," ordered Hal.

Another click from another gun immediately followed.

"And your partner best not get any ideas either," Morty joined in.

Hal and Morty entered the clearing with guns aimed at Ab and Del. A look of horror and surprise came upon Morty when he saw the prisoner shot dead, still tied to the tree.

"He was shot accidental," explained John. "I'll fill you in later."

"I show hate ta see that. I was hoping to get a piece of him myself," said Hal.

"I'm sure glad to see you two," said John.

"You can thank Hal for that. He's the one who saw these two buzzards tailing you."

"I'm much obliged to you both. You can maybe escort these gentlemen back to town with Miller's body. Turn in your bill for his burying and I'll see to it the government pays it."

"We can do that."

"At the first telegraph I come to, I'll make out all the

reports on him."

The mention of the telegraph reminded Morty of the one in his pocket. He handed it to John.

"This came for you, but you had done left town."

John took it and stuck it in his pocket.

Hal sent Gilbert and Bunckus to retrieve the horses. While John and Morty covered the bounty hunters, he cut Miller loose. It didn't take long for the boys to return with all the animals.

"How do you propose to haul that body back?" asked Ab.

"I'm ona tie him cross yo hoss."

"You will do no such thing!"

"I show am. You won't need it, cause you gonna be walking."

"What!"

"You heard me. Now, you and yo buddy git ova dare and hep load em on."

Morty dropped the saddles from the two horses and put them and the saddlebags into the wagon. John informed the two would-be bounty hunters that he would leave their gear and their guns with the sheriff in Rico, adding they would only be able to get them back with a letter from Morty.

After securing the corpse, Hal went to work on Ab and Del. He removed the handcuffs from Miller and, with Morty's pair, cuffed their hands behind their back. He then took some of the rope and made a noose for each of them. He placed the noose around their necks and ran the excess down the back and under the handcuffs. Then, he looped the rope around the horns of his and Morty's saddles. When the ropes were pulled the men's heads were drawn back and their hands were drawn upward. John had never seen anything like it.

"You can't march us all the way to town like this," protested Del.

"We can and we is," answered Hal.

"If we trip we could break our necks."

"Then I suggest you best not trip," added Morty. He was starting to like his job.

"Marshal, all the best to you. Gilbert, where are you boys going?"

"I guess wees gonna take Marshal John to tha next town so's he can ketch a train home."

The group said their final goodbyes and then Hal and Morty started back to Silverton with the bounty hunters in front and their horses, with Miller, following behind. As they left the clearing, Del lamented the situation.

"We got nothing. Nothing! A worthless dead man and a fortune in gold…lost…gone forever!"

THIRTY SEVEN

Gilbert watched until the Morty and company were out of sight, then he turned to John.

"Marshal John, it ain't lost."

"What are you talking about?" asked John.

"At gold...I don't thank it's lost."

"Why do you say that?" quizzed John.

"Was it heavy gold bars?"

"That's what I understand." John's expression was serious.

"I thank it's under ire cabin, or where ire cabin used ta be."

Shock, panic, and amazement swept over John. He wanted to believe what he had just heard, but it was far too incredible. It couldn't be true. But, wasn't it worth a look?

"Let's get a fire going and make some coffee. I packed a little grub, maybe we can have some breakfast. Give those guys time to get ahead of us, and then we will go back to your cabin and take a look."

John stalled around for about an hour and a half. As the boys enjoyed breakfast, he took time to read the telegraph message. He was taken aback by the revelation that Miller had returned with the intent of trapping and finishing him.

"Thank you, Lord," came across his mind. It was his third prayer within the past twenty four hours.

Breakfast ended and they started for the boys' former dwelling. Traveling was faster now that the horses were refreshed, the wagon was lighter, and the road back was more downhill. Three hours later they arrived at the pile of ashes that used to be the cabin. Bunckus and Gilbert led the Marshal straight to a spot at the northeast corner and started kicking away the rubble.

Under the ashes and beneath a few inches of soil they uncovered a strongbox. John could not believe his eyes. He removed the lid, pulled back the burlap lining, and exposed the pristine bullion bars. There were nine whole ones and half of another.

John rose up and surveyed the area for the first time. He noticed then, that where they were standing was almost directly below the Ophir road. The scar of its cutting through the mountain was visible in the distance. It would not have been too difficult to lead a mule down the mountain with the load. This would also explain the missing mule from the robbery. It had been a team of four, but only three were found at the scene of the crime.

"When did you find it?"

"Right after we moved in here. Bunckus saw some of the floorboards was loose and got ta lookin' under 'em. He noticed that dirt was loose too and after scratchin' a bit he uncovered it."

"You boys have been here a year, starving and freezing, while sleeping on top of a king's ransom in gold? Why didn't you take it?"

"It weren't none of ires," answered Gilbert.

John would never have believed the story if it had been told to him. He was witness to the poverty of these two dregs of society. Now, he was in awe of their honesty. They could have made off with the treasure and no one would have been the wiser. He stood silent for a moment, trying to absorb the revelation.

"Ya see Marshal, the Good Lord wouldn't never bless us if we took what didn't blong to us."

"Boys, I must say, I'm shocked. I don't know of anybody else who would have been so honest. Listen to me carefully now…part of this is yours…or it will be."

"Whatcha mean?"

"Well, there will be a reward for turning it back in."

Bunckus and Gilbert stared open-mouthed at each other.

"Really, Marshal? How much?"

"I don't know just yet. Let's get it loaded and take it to Ophir. They'll weigh it up and we will find out."

It took the rest of the day to reach the small mining town of Ophir. Hard times had hit it like all the others. Several of the businesses on Main Street were boarded up. John stopped the wagon at the local sheriff's office. Darkness was settling in, but the coal oil lamp from within told him someone was inside.

He left the boys in the wagon with strict orders to remain quiet, especially about the cargo. In a few minutes the sheriff came out and hurriedly helped to get the gold inside and locked in a cell. It took a while to get the local banker and some of the owners of the mine to the jail. Once all were present, John told them the story. Their joy was uncontrollable. They never thought to ever see it again; some never did.

A few of the miners had everything they owned tied up in this shipment; when it was lost, so was their hope and future. Some gave up and left the area, never to be heard from again. Two of them took their own lives out of despair.

John told the boys to return to the wagon while he talked business. At the current price, the load was valued at

$76000.00. The owners started with an offer of three percent reward, but after John's persuasion and his threat of confiscating it until a thorough investigation was made, they settled on five. Instead of cash or bank draft, John also persuaded them to weigh out the reward in gold from the bars. The amount was $3800.00.

John took the gold, placed it in a bag and stuffed it in his pocket. He also explained that Bunckus and Gilbert were still deputized and that they would stay the night in the jail and keep watch. This was agreed to, so all went home to spread the news. When all were gone, John brought the boys in and informed them of what they had. The celebration was not quite what John expected.

Instead of dancing and shouting, they just held each other and cried. Their tears were mixed with several expressions of praise and thanks to God. John had never seen anyone like these two.

"Ain't God good, Marshal John?" asked Gilbert.

John hesitated, "Yes, I suppose He is."

"Can you hep figger how much ten percent of this reward is?"

"Ten percent is $380.00."

"Dang Bunckus, you yere at? We get ta pay $380.00 in

tithes!"

"You're going to what?" queried John. "You boys been living near starvation most of your lives and you're going to give that much money to a preacher?"

"Marshal, if we don't do ire money right, God ain't gonna bless it."

"And what if some preacher just wastes it?"

"Well, at's between him and the good Lord. Ya got ta pay ya tithes, Marshal John."

John did not wish to discuss it further; he had little time or patience for some of the ministers he had met.

THIRTY EIGHT

The boys were up early and ready to leave for the town of Dolores. They were still a bit dazed at their change of fortune. They were in the wagon waiting for John when he left the jail.

"You boys don't need to take me to Dolores, I can borrow a horse. I still plan to pay you boys what I promised too."

"Aw, we got to go down there anyways, Marshal. We need to pay off at marker."

John had heard a lot about this mysterious marker, so he was curious to see the end of it."

"Much obliged." He climbed on and away they went.

"Oh, and Marshal John, you don't owe us nothin'."

John started to protest, but he noticed the immense pride Gilbert had in not feeling destitute for the first time in his life.

"Much obliged."

Several hours and curves brought them to the town of Dolores on the banks of the river by the same name. Gilbert steered the wagon to the far side of town and halted in front of a stone cutter's shop. The owner was seated out front on a low stool as he chiseled away on a new millstone. He bent his head down to peer above his thick glasses.

"I had done about give up on you two. It took you this long to make forty dollars?"

"Yes sir, wees sorry hit took so long. Have ya got tha marker done?"

"It's been done. I got it out back. Come on."

Gilbert, Bunckus, and John followed the man through his shop and out to a storeroom in the rear of the place. There, in a corner by itself, stood a two-inch thick granite slab about three feet high and eighteen inches wide. The stone cutter removed the covering and revealed the inscription. It was a single word.

"Is that what you wanted on it?"

"What's it say, Marshal?"

John looked at the simple wording.

"It says, 'HERE'…that's it…it just says, 'HERE'."

"That's what you ordered, wasn't it?"

"Yes sir, at's perfect."

John was more mystified than ever about this marker. He had to know the rest of it. The three of them loaded the stone.

"Marshal John, we'll take ya to tha train and then head out. We sure are glad to have met ya," said Gilbert.

"Now just hold on a minute. You got to explain to me this headstone. When I heard you boys saying you had to pay off a marker, I didn't know you meant a grave marker."

"Well, if ya want to ride with us, we tell ya about on the way."

John agreed and they headed out of town to the northwest. Along the way Gilbert explained how he and Bunckus were traveling to Wyoming to look for work on one of the cattle ranches there. He shared their time in Oklahoma tending cattle for various ranchers. Bunckus, he said, had a natural gift for taking care of calves. He told of their reaching one of the crossings of the Dolores River and discovering an abandoned wagon. In fact, it was the one they were riding in.

"They weren't no horse or folks nowhere's. I was gonna look up and down the river, but Bunckus yelled at he'd fount a baby in the wagon. I run back and sure 'nuff it was."

"A baby?"

"Yes sir, a little girl, and she was bad sick…had a real high fever. We couldn't find her folks, so we hitched ire horse to the wagon and turned back to town to see if we could git a doctor. Poor little thang died though. Bunckus tried everthang he knew. She was just too sick."

Bunckus began tearing up as he relived the day.

"We stopped and cleaned her up as best we could. Bunckus found one of her little outfits and dressed her. We wrapped her in a blanket, dug her a proper grave and buried her just off the road.

John felt an emotion forming within him; an emotion he though was gone forever. There was a lump forming in his throat. He had to wait a bit before he spoke.

"So, you boys thought she needed a marker too?"

"Yes sir. Bunckus was afraid that the Lord wouldn't be able to find her when he comes back; her being so little in nis great big ole desert."

"You didn't consider letting someone else take care of it?"

"Ain't nobody else knowd where she was."

John remained silent for the rest of the journey. His entire adult life had spent dealing with some of the worst of society. He had seen his share of self-proclaimed righteous folks, but this was his first encounter with anyone who actually lived their faith.

They finally reached the spot. The boys had erected a small cairn to mark it. John helped set the marker and bowed his head while Gilbert offered a final prayer. With no more to be done, they returned to town. John wept. The trio entered town as the last rays of sun were filtering across the buildings. They got rooms for the night and some well-needed rest.

Early the next morning, John sent a message to Morty that all was well. He also sent messages to all parties involved that the ordeal with D.H. Miller was closed. He messaged Sheriff Keating and Dr. Clark, with a promise to give them the full story by letter as soon as he got home.

The Stick Brothers were faithful to their promise of tithing. They went to the bank and converted $380.00 worth of gold into cash and stopped at the first church they came to. The pastor could only cry for the answered prayer. He informed the boys that the church was about to close due to not being able to meet its debt.

Their tithe more than covered the need. Everyone rejoiced. They had decided to take the train to Wyoming, so they gave the wagon and horses to the church also, with a promise they would donate to a family in need. John was puzzled again by these two when he saw them come into the station, on foot, carrying a butter churn.

"Marshal John, all the stuff in that wagon we fount got burnt up in ire cabin. The only thang we saved was is churn.

It's got some papers in it, but we cain't read. Will you take it and maybe find out if they are any good?"

"I'll do what I can."

An idea sprang into John's mind. He had not planned it, but was helpless to stop himself from asking.

"You boys ever think about buying you a place in Arizona Territory?"

"Naw sir. Is it nice?"

"I like it. It's not Wyoming cattle country, but you can raise a small spread there."

The boys liked the idea and promptly bought tickets. This time though, John took care to explain the ticket punching process to them. The conductor called for all to board and in a very few minutes, John Law was finally going home.

EPILOGUE

Three weeks later John sat with his feet propped on the rail of his back porch watching the sun slowly sink behind the hills. To his right sat Joan, with her feet propped as well. A mile away, Bunckus and Gilbert sat in the open flap of their new canvas tent watching the same view. They had just this day, with John's help, finalized all the papers on a one hundred acre parcel of land. The tent was set up until a house could be built. This was their first sunset in a place they could call their own.

Further east and further south, Sheriff Albert Keating and Matt Clark were in Juarez looking up Padron. His former business was closed. They eventually found him at home watching the sunset. Albert gave him the whole story of Miller. Padron listened silently until he was finished.

"Sheriff, it is good that this bad man is gone, but I don't have hate for him like before. Old Padron, he try to change."

"We noticed your bar is closed."

"Yes, I close down. That place help hurt lot of people. I can no longer do that. Understand Sheriff, I am not a saint. Old Padron though, he just not as big a devil as he used to be."

"I suppose we could all maybe improve a little," said

Albert.

"Can you believe Sheriff, I go back to church now? I even try to learn to pray. Are you praying man Sheriff?"

The question made him uncomfortable. "I need to be I guess."

"What of you Dr. Clark? You pray?"

"No, I am a man of reason. If I can't see it, or touch it, I don't believe in it."

"You ever have thoughts or dreams, Doctor?"

"Well, sure."

"Then, are they real?"

Matt did not answer. All three men remained silent and watched the sunset.

Far to the north, in the empty wilderness on the western edge of Colorado, the last rays of sunset bathed its crimson-orange glow across a single word chiseled into a solitary, granite marker.

www.ingramcontent.com/pod-product-compliance
Lightning Source LLC
Chambersburg PA
CBHW031957240626
47153CB00003B/1013